inside girl

PERFECT MATCH

Also by J. Minter:

the insiders series

the insiders

pass it on

take it off

break every rule

hold on tight

girls we love

the inside girl series

inside girl

the sweetest thing

some kind of wonderful

all that glitters

a novel by J. MINTER

author of the insiders

New York • Berlin • London

Published by Bloomsbury U.S.A. Children's Books
175 Fifth Avenue, New York, NY 10010

Library of Congress Cataloging-in-Publication Data
Minter, J.
Perfect match : an inside girl novel / J. Minter. — 1st U.S. ed.
p. cm.
Summary: As Valentine's Day approaches and her friends have called a boycott on boys, high-schooler Flan decides to dabble in matchmaking so all her friends can enjoy the upcoming dance.
ISBN-13: 978-1-59990-335-4 • ISBN-10: 1-59990-335-0
[1. Dating (Social customs)—Fiction. 2. Friendship—Fiction. 3. Valentine's Day—Fiction. 4. New York (N.Y.)—Fiction.] I. Title.
PZ7.M67334Go 2009 [Fic]—dc22 2008039176

Produced by Alloy Entertainment
151 West 26th Street, New York, NY 10001

First U.S. Edition 2009
Printed in the U.S.A. by Quebecor World Fairfield
10 9 8 7 6 5 4 3 2 1

All papers used by Bloomsbury U.S.A. are natural, recyclable products made from wood grown in well-managed forests. The manufacturing processes conform to the environmental regulations of the country of origin.

for Jordan, future heartbreaker

inside girl

PERFECT MATCH

YA F MIN
1476 0956
Minter, J.
LCL

Chapter 1

OUT OF RANGE

Outside, behind the velvet rope on Houston Street, the winding crowd I'd just zipped past looked cold. But inside, at a private Screen Actors Guild party in the famously mod Angelika theater, things were getting hot, hot, hot.

"I want you to meet my girlfriend, Flan."

I know, I know, these words have been said about me before. I'll be the first to admit that I've had my fair share of boyfriends. But truthfully, the introduction had never sounded so sweet as it did when it was uttered by Alex Altfest, the Prince of New York, whose arm was lovingly curved around my waist.

We were standing in the glittering atrium of the theater, all dressed up to attend this very choice Hollywood-style event—made even more choice by the fact that it was hosted by one of Alex's friends to celebrate the premiere of his new film, *Cache Creek*.

The Angelika is most Manhattanites' destination for taking in classic artsy flicks—from foreign shorts to Woody Allen revivals. I loved seeing movies there, but until tonight I'd never thought about it as a hot spot for Hollywood types. With its high glass ceilings, multilevel cocktail bar, and black-tie waiter service, the Angelika really felt like a place to see and be seen. Which is why I was glad I'd decided to wear my new sapphire Tory Burch heels—and why I was even gladder to have the Prince of New York on my arm. I sighed contentedly and leaned into Alex.

"Flan?" Alex said, giving me a sideways grin.

Oh, right, introductions. I probably wasn't making a dazzling first impression by gazing off introspectively.

"This is my old crew from lacrosse camp—Brady, Saxton, and Phil. Brady's the one I told you about, the producer for *Cache Creek*." Alex moved his arm to my shoulders. "Guys, this is her."

The way he said it—*this is her*—like he'd spent enough time talking about me that his friends could now put my face to the girl in his stories—well, it sort of made me glow inside. I mean, I talked about Alex all the time to my friends, but until then, I hadn't considered that he might do the same thing.

Brady stuck out his hand. He was almost as tall as

Alex, with curly dark hair and dimples. "We've heard lots about you." He nodded at Alex. "In fact, it's kinda hard to get this guy to *stop* talking about you."

I could feel myself blushing. "I've heard good things about you, too," I said, taking a flute of acai spritzer from a passing waiter's tray. "Alex says the movie's getting lots of buzz."

"Nah," Saxton piped in, shrugging dramatically. He was blond and muscular with intense green eyes. "It was only *the* movie at Sundance last month, no big deal."

"And Brady only has Scorsese on his knees to direct his next film," Phil said, punching Brady's shoulder. "When are you going to break the news that you cast me as the lead?"

"Maybe when I find an actress worthy of your Yale drama school degree." Brady laughed. "Or at least one the studio can bank on, considering you're not exactly a household name." Brady shrugged apologetically as Phil feigned offense.

I was pretty impressed that Alex was friends with such a talented, artsy group of guys. Of course, I did have my token film-star best friend, Sara-Beth Benny. But SBB's movies weren't exactly the kind that got airtime at the Angelika. Although she had been moaning to me lately about her agent wanting her to do a project to up her dramatic cred—i.e., not another of her famous teenybopper blockbusters.

Hmm . . . If Brady was already working on another film, maybe I could find a way to introduce them? Not that SBB didn't already have an agent and a PR team and four personal assistants . . . but it'd be so cool to hook her up with a connection who could help her career. I'd mention it to Alex later.

Alex squeezed my shoulder. "Come on, I want to show you around."

As we mingled throughout the cocktail hour, I was struck by how great and attentive Alex was being. Even though he seemed to know everyone, he never left my side. As he spun me around the room for introductions, I got the feeling that a lot of people were sizing me—and my Tory Burch heels—up.

I'd been to enough parties and premieres to handle the scrutinizing gazes of the rich and fashion-conscious. Even so, there was something new about being introduced as one half of a couple. I wasn't used to it—my boy life and my socialite life had always been kind of separate entities in the past. But with Alex periodically planting his lips on my cheek and whispering funny details about all the people I was meeting—"that guy makes his driver take him to McDonald's in the Bronx so his nutritionist wife won't find out he eats meat"—I realized I was totally into being his other half.

"This is amazing." I turned to Alex, after I'd met more people than I could remember. "I'm so glad you invited me."

He smiled. "You're going to be even more glad when I tell you who else I invited."

I must have looked confused, because Alex spun me toward the entryway. My best friend, Camille, and her new boyfriend, Xander, were walking up the steps, hand in hand!

"Brady gave me two extra tickets to the screening at the last minute," Alex said. "Thought you might like to see a familiar face in the crowd."

"Hey, lovebirds," Camille called, flipping her trademark long gold hair. "Swank party, Alex. Ooh, swankier shoes, Flan. Bendel's?" she asked.

"Scoop," I corrected.

"Well, now that that important matter's settled," Xander joked, "should we watch this movie or what?"

The boys put their arms around us and our foursome joined the glittering, black-clad crowd at the doors to the theater. The only thing better than Xander finally asking Camille out was the fact that Xander and Alex went way back to their days at Little Red Schoolhouse, so they were almost as tight as Camille and me.

"We definitely have to start double-dating more often," I whispered to Camille as we entered the theater.

"I *know*," Camille said. "Friend time and boy time at the *same* time. What's better?"

The theater was already packed, and everyone was rushing to claim seats. As a friend of the producer, Alex had a group of reserved seats right in the middle. The four of us were able to sit down and relax with no problem, just in time to catch the scene unfolding in the row ahead of us.

A barrel-chested, bald man in Prada shoes and a tight pink T-shirt that read *Don't Mess with the Diva* had spread out his winter gear across four empty seats and was watching over them like a hawk.

"Um, excuse me," an equally muscular bald guy said to him in a huffy voice. "Where do you think you are, the high school lunchroom? You can't save seats in a New York City movie theater."

"I can if you knew who my friends are," Muscles Number One said defiantly, crossing his arms over his chest.

"That doesn't even make any *sense*," Muscles Two scoffed.

Camille and I looked at each other with raised eyebrows and I bit my lip to keep from laughing. It was a favorite secret pastime of ours—eavesdropping on Chelsea boys in catfights. Sometimes we staked out the back table at the Pinkberry on Eighth Avenue just to see what kind of drama we could witness.

But these two dudes were getting serious about the seats. One of them was rolling up his sleeves like he was about to throw a punch. That only happened at Pinkberry when they ran out of mochi. Just when I thought things were going to get ugly, Muscles Two said: "Wait a minute—you look familiar." He squinted at his opponent. "Did you do that Calvin Klein ad on the back of the M16 bus?"

Muscles One shrugged. "Maybe."

"Ohmigod, huge fan," Muscles Two said, making the I'm-not-worthy motion with his arms. Changing his tack, he sized up his opponent. "How about if I agree to find another seat, you agree to give me your number?"

Next to Camille, Xander leaned in to whisper, "You guys are so eating this up, aren't you?"

I giggled under my breath.

"Like it's Pinkberry," Camille replied.

"I guess love is in the air," Alex said, squeezing my hand.

He was right. Valentine's Day was a little over a week away. Even though I had a boyfriend, and so should probably have given the holiday some thought, I was mostly aware of how close it was because of my single friends at Thoney. They were already complaining about how depressing the whole month of February was unless you had a valentine.

I'd thought my friends were being dramatic, but maybe it was exactly this fear of spending February fourteenth alone that stopped the guys in front of us from clocking each other. Maybe Cupid made them take out their Palms to exchange numbers instead.

Just before the lights dimmed, Muscles Two snapped a photo of Muscles One on his phone. "Text me!" he grinned, before shuffling off to his seat.

"Classic New York," Camille said, whipping her hair into a giant bun and putting on her glasses to assume her I'm-watching-a-movie pose.

From the opening scene of the film, I was hooked—and even more impressed by Brady. It was the story of two star-crossed lovers, separated by distance, and family obligations, and some really incredible costume changes. *Hmm, I wonder where the lead actress got that belt. . . .*

But after a few minutes, I found myself distracted by a faint blue light in front of me. When I leaned forward, I realized that it was the glowing cell phone of Muscles One. How rude. Was he already texting

Muscles Two? Maybe if I leaned forward just a little bit more, I could make out what they were saying. It was bound to be hilariously racy. A little further . . . a little further . . . *ooph*! Before I realized what was happening, I'd fallen out of my seat. Everyone around us turned to look at me and held their fingers up to their lips.

"Shhhhhh," Muscles One said to me brusquely. Like he was paying *so* much attention to the movie!

Oh well, it served me right. I looked at Alex, who was shaking his head with a knowing smirk. I shrugged in apology, took his hand, and vowed to get back into watching the movie. No more spying!

But a few minutes later, I was distracted again by the distinct buzz of a vibrating cell phone. Now this guy was really being rude! But when the buzzing didn't stop, I realized that I was the culprit this time. Whoops.

In an attempt to be smooth, I reached down to turn it off. But before the screen went black, I noticed that I had four missed calls and three text messages from the girls in my Thoney clique. I couldn't help taking a quick glance.

From Harper: PARTY AT VANS. WE'RE ALL GOING.

From Amory: I'M GOING TO RICKY'S FOR PRIMPING PROPS. WHO WANTS GLITTER EYE SHADOW?

From Morgan: MEET ON THE CORNER OF PERRY AND WEST FOURTH. I HAVE THE CODE TO GET UPSTAIRS.

I looked over at Camille; I was sure the girls would have texted her as well. But she didn't seem to know or care about it. I kind of envied that she was able to focus on the movie. I was having a great time too, but now that I knew that all my friends were heading out to a party and assuming that I'd meet them there . . . well, my mind was sort of wandering. Should I let them know where I was? Would they be bummed that I couldn't make it? *Could* I make it, if we went right after the movie?

Wait, what was I thinking? It was just a party. I'd missed parties before and survived to tell about it. And here I was, at this amazingly fun event, with *Alex*, who I adored and who'd been cool enough to invite my best friend to join us.

Come on, Flan. Everyone in New York was looking for love and Cupid was actively smiling down on me. What more could I ask for?

Chapter 2

DON'T KNOCK IT TILL YOU MOCKET

Early the next morning, I met Camille and SBB for brunch at a tiny East Village restaurant called Prune. They don't take reservations, so you have to get there right when the doors open at ten o'clock if you want to avoid standing in line for an hour. But they do have the best breakfast BLTs in the city, so it's definitely worth the early rising.

Luckily, all three of us arrived at the same time and SBB only had to sign three autographs and pose for two photographers on the way in, so we were able to snag our favorite sunny table under the hanging ivy plant by the window. The crowd was young and beautiful, mostly couples or small groups of girls. Each place setting contained the classic brunch trifecta: a frothy cappuccino, a pair of aviator sunglasses, and a PDA. The other groups of girls were all laughing as they dished out their tales of the weekend's adventures, but I noticed that the vibe at most of the couples' tables was decidedly lower key.

"Is it me," I asked, smearing some of Prune's signature blood orange marmalade on a hunk of whole-grain toast, "or do the girls-only cliques seem to be having way more fun than the girls who are here with their boyfriends?"

"Probably because it's more fun to talk smack about your boyfriend to your friends than it is to actually hang out with him," SBB said thoughtfully, biting into her black bean flapjacks.

"Whoa, where did that come from?" Camille asked. "Is something going on between you and JR?"

SBB threw her head back in a laugh. "Not even. Jake Riverdale and I are more in love than ever. It's called *empathy*," she said, sounding out each syllable. Camille and I shared a secret smirk as SBB continued her explanation. "It's an acting term where you put yourself in someone else's shoes. I've been working on it recently at my agent's suggestion." She glanced around the room. "Take that couple over there." SBB nodded to her left at a couple so lifeless, they practically looked asleep. "Wouldn't you be Somber Sally if you were dating that dude? Wouldn't you rather be hanging with . . ." She scanned the room until her eyes landed on a group of girls practically falling out of their chairs with that laugh specifi

"Them?"

I was used to SBB's "acting" terms

having been BFFs with the teen actress *Rolling*

had recently called "an intergalactic star" since we were both wearing training bras. But today, SBB's professional lingo made me wonder about life off-screen.

"Isn't it possible," I asked the girls, "to have as much fun with your boyfriend as with your friends?"

"Sometimes it seems like a lot more is at stake with boys," Camille said, looking down at her plate. "Like every word you say to each other *means* something, you know? It's easier to navigate when things happen with your girlfriends than with your boyfriend."

"Okay, your turn," I said to Camille. "I know you don't have SBB's excuse that your working on your act. Is everything okay with Xander? You guys seemed so good last night."

"We were. We are," she sighed, popping the last bite of her asparagus quiche in her mouth. "But after we left you guys at the movie, we both had messages from our friends to go to separate parties. And he wanted to go meet up with them and I didn't. I just got scared that I might be more into him than he is into me." She looked at me. "Do you know what I mean?"

The truth was, Alex and I had had the exact opposite conversation last night after the movie. But I knew that just because I thought it would be fun to meet up with friends after the movie, it didn't mean that I wasn't totally into Alex—and looking at Camille now, I was sure that the case was the same for Xander.

"Oh, you girls and your little worries!" SBB laughed, picking up the check. "I won't hear any more of it. You're beautiful and adored by your men, *capisce*?"

"Nice empathy, SBB," I joked.

"Empathize this: what we need is some retail therapy. Now, who knows what she's getting her man for Valentine's Day? *That*, ladies, is something worth stressing over."

As we stepped out of the warm, cozy restaurant into the harsh reality of February in New York, all three of us hustled into our hats and mittens. SBB whistled for a cab.

"Bloomingdale's on Broadway," she told the driver. Then she pulled out a thick packet of paper bound like a screenplay with three golden brads. But I doubted that anyone would title a script SHOPPING LIST. "What?" She shrugged at us. "I don't mess around with it comes to retail therapy."

When the cab pulled up to the great white building,

SBB got out first and started calling out a breakdown of the floor plan. "Boys first. We'll start at the third floor and move through the fifth. Then, once we've gotten the gift-buying work out of the way, we can reward ourselves with spa treatments on six and shoes on four."

Wow, it usually took me an hour just to make it out of the cosmetics section on the ground floor at Bloomingdale's. Since I had no good ideas about what to get Alex for Valentine's Day, I was pretty grateful that I had SBB-on-a-mission to keep me on track.

While we thumbed through piles of men's shirts and racks of ties and boxes of cuff links, I could feel my eyes glazing over. It's not that I wasn't interested in shopping for Alex—though I had to admit, high-heeled boots were way more fun to look at than cuff links. I mean, what *were* cuff links, anyway? But I just didn't think any of this stuff was quite right for Alex. And I wanted to get him something really special. What exactly that was going to be just hadn't come to me yet.

I looked at Camille to see if she was having any more luck. Her brow was furrowed in frustration.

"It's not just finding a Valentine's present that I'm worried about," she explained when she saw the concerned look on my face. She was holding up a hideously ugly brown sweater without even seeming to see it. "Xander's birthday is the week after next, *and* our one-month anniversary is right after that, but I don't want to go overboard with the gifts—especially if he doesn't think that one month is a big anniversary, 'cause you know, some guys don't really think about that, and—"

I had never seen Camille so unglued over a guy. I could always count on her to be the smart, balanced, carefree one. What was making her so nervous? I looped my arm through hers.

"Maybe you should follow SBB's lead," I suggested. "Put yourself in her shoes. Look at her. She's dating the most popular pop star on the planet and the only thing in her relationship that she's not completely confident about is whether JR would prefer the blue or the green Burberry scarf. You should get Xander what feels right. Try not to overthink it."

She nodded. "You're right." Her eyes finally locked on the mess of brown merino wool in her hands. "God, what am I doing with this awful sweater? Yuck. This is certainly *not* the answer." She tossed it back in the sale bin and sighed. "I'm going to go check out those money clips over there."

"Good idea." I smiled. Relieved that Camille seemed to have found her purpose, I looked around for a bench. It might have been the first time in my life that I opted out of shopping. I felt a little bit like my dad or brother when Mom, Feb, and I dragged them around department stores.

"Eeeek!" SBB came up from behind me and grabbed my shoulders. "Flan, thank you *so* much!"

"For what?" I asked, confused.

"For revitalizing my entire career!" She was bouncing on her Ferragamo heels. The last time I'd heard her so breathless, she'd just hurled herself over one of the blue *Village Voice* newspaper displays on West Broadway to avoid a Segway-riding paparazzo across the street. "Alex's friend, Brody? Or Brindy? Or, oh, Brady! Well, he just *inquired* about me. He got my agent's name from Alex . . . and he wants to audition me for a part! In his new indie film! Can you believe it? My agent said the script is totally smart and edgy. So it's basically the opposite of anything I've done before. It'll be groundbreaking! It'll be revolutionary! It'll be—"

"That's so great, SBB," I said. I was thrilled for her—and more than a little thrilled with Alex. I'd only mentioned SBB's career concerns in passing after the movie. It was totally sweet and perceptive of him to talk to Brady already, and without me even having to ask.

"So what's the movie about?" I asked. "What role are you auditioning for?"

"Oh, you know, it's a gritty drama, set in an all-American high school. And I would play the typical high school student. I'll just have to channel my inner—oh *no*! My career is finished!"

The color drained from her face and she sank onto the bench next to me.

"What is it?" I asked, holding her small body upright. I started to fan her with my mittens. "What's wrong?"

Very slowly, my little starlet eked out the words. "I never went to high school. I have no experience with 'typical.' I don't have a chance." SBB sighed wistfully.

I suppressed a grin. "SBB, high school is easy."

She looked at me doubtfully.

"Okay," I reconsidered. "It's not easy to *live* through, but I promise you, it will be a breeze for you to act. It's all your favorite stuff—boys, fashion, immeasurable drama." I patted her knee. "Trust me, with my help, you'll be the most convincing high school student the silver screen has ever seen."

SBB's eyes got all wide and dewy, the way they did when she felt really moved. "You'll help me, Flannie? I really want to prove that I can do this. I want to become a legitimate indie drama darling, the toast of the Independent Spirit Awards."

"Lucky for you," I said, "I'm something of an expert on high school drama. You can put your empathy skills to use on me."

As SBB gave me a tight side squeeze, Camille reappeared in front of us. "So," she said tantalizingly, holding her hands behind her back. "What do we think of this?" She held up a pocket watch dangling from a cool, sort of gaudy gold rope. "When you open it up," she explained while demonstrating, "there are three different compartments. The watch is one, and you can store two pictures on the sides. It's kind of a like a functional man locket. Weird or cool?"

"It's a mocket!" SBB squealed. "It's perfect! Where'd you find it? We'll take three, right, Flan?"

Camille led us over to the glass case where she'd found the golden mockets. I wasn't so sure this screamed *Alex*, but the other girls seemed so into it that I didn't want to argue. As the two of them brainstormed exactly which photos they'd put inside the lockets, I felt my phone buzz in my bag. It was a text from Morgan, whom I realized I hadn't seen all weekend.

YOU ALIVE? BEEN MISSING YOUR PRETTY FACE, she wrote. GRAB A COFFEE?

Morgan lived in SoHo, within walking distance from Bloomingdale's, so it'd be super easy for her to come meet up with us. But as I looked at my two friends gushing over their mockets, I tried to imagine Morgan hanging out in the men's section. All we were doing was talking about and shopping for our boyfriends. Of all my single friends, she seemed the most sensitive about her lack of significant other. I didn't want to blow her off, so I texted back:

HOW 'BOUT LATTES TOMORROW BEFORE SCHOOL? WE'LL NEED THE CAFFEINE TO GET THROUGH ANOTHER MONDAY

I knew I was doing Morgan a favor by opting to devote time to her solo, but something about my response felt a little forced. When had it started feeling like I had to dole out time with my friends based on whether or not they had boyfriends?

"Flan," SBB called me back to reality. "We're about to check out. You want in on the mocket, right?"

"Okay," I surrendered, feeling more enthusiastic about getting out of the men's department than about the gift itself. "Yes, I'll take the mocket." I was going to need some serious time in the shoe section to recover from this retail therapy session.

Chapter 3

SWEET MISFORTUNE

A few hours later, I was holed up in my bedroom, avoiding my chemistry homework and holding up the mocket I'd just bought for Alex for the approval of my very discriminating Pomeranian, Noodles.

He was curled up in my arms, making his contented half-snore, half-purr sound (anyone who's met Noodles can attest to the fact that he must have been a cat in a former life). But when I showed him the mocket, his head perked up and he sniffed it suspiciously.

"It's all wrong, isn't it?" I asked, nuzzling his face.

Noodles barked twice in the affirmative. I lay back on my bed and sighed. It was a week and a half until Valentine's Day and after many hours of shopping for Alex I was back at square one. What's more, I was feeling incapable of taking my own advice to Camille. I felt like so much was riding on this gift. Since our relationship was pretty new and I was still trying to feel things out, I just wanted to make sure to do everything right. The pressure was really starting to get to me.

A knock at my door interrupted my thoughts. "Flan?" My father stuck his head in. "We're ordering from Chin-Chin," he said. "You want the usual?"

Before he'd even finished his question, I had leapt from my bed to fling my arms around him. "Dad! When did you get back in town?"

More often than not, the rest of my family's professional globe-trotting duties left me sole proprietor of our way-too-big-for-one-girl town house in the West Village.

My dad shrugged. "Bolivia was way too hot for your mother. We flew back this afternoon."

It only took one look at my father to know that he spent very little time in the city during the winter. His neatly trimmed blond hair framed a face too tan for February in New York. His most recent hobby was buying mansions in foreign countries, declaring them fixer-uppers, and spending all his time renovating them. So whenever my parents made an appearance at our house, it was always cause for celebration.

"That beats the leftover pizza feast I had planned," I said, breathing in the familiar piney smell of my dad's aftershave. "I thought I was home alone."

"Far from it." My dad smiled, ruffling my hair. "We've got a full house, kiddo. Patch got in this afternoon from L.A. and he's meeting Feb at the airport as we speak. I think they're each bringing a *friend* home for dinner."

"They're not calling them *friends* anymore, Richard." I heard my mother's voice coming up the stairs. "You're so old-fashioned." She cupped my face in her cool, manicured hands and kissed both my cheeks. "Hello, darling," she said. "Isn't the new PC word for one's significant other *partner*? That's what Whoopi calls her boyfriend on *The View*."

"Wait," I said, trying to catch up to my in-on-all-the-family-gossip parents. "Patch and Feb suddenly have partners? And they're bringing them to dinner? Why didn't anyone tell me?"

My mother clucked her tongue. "Have you lost your flair for the impromptu dinner party? Didn't your father and I teach you anything? Have we been away too long?"

"No, yes, and yes," I said. "I'm so glad you guys are back, even if it's only for—"

My dad looked at his watch. "Fourteen hours. Why don't you give Alex a call? See if he wants in on this partners evening?"

When my parents went downstairs to get ready for

dinner, I slid the mocket into my underwear drawer and picked up my phone to text Alex.

DINNER PLANS? CAN I TEMPT YOU WITH GREASY CHINESE FOOD AND MY FAMILY?

I was trying to sound casual, since I knew it was a really last-minute invitation, but when Alex replied: WISH I COULD! COMMITTED TO GRANDMA'S TASTELESS CHICKEN TONIGHT, I couldn't help feeling a little bit bummed. My family was together so rarely that I hated missing the opportunity to have Alex at my side. Especially if Patch and Feb were both bringing home their, uh, *partners*.

Oh well—dinner with the fam, even as the seventh wheel, still beat microwaved pizza.

Soon a mess of voices filtered up from the first floor and I rushed down to meet my siblings, whom I hadn't seen in over a month. When I saw my older sister tripping over her suitcases in the foyer, a big smile spread across my face—then quickly turned into a laugh.

Feb was decked out in head-to-toe safari gear. A tall, blond guy standing with his arm around her sported a coordinating ensemble.

"So that's what you've been doing all month—hunting for ivory?" I joked, giving Feb a kiss.

"Not exactly," she said, shoving one of three massive

trunks against the wall. “Kelly and I just started a line of activewear with Karl Lagerfeld. It’s inspired by the haute Australian bush hunter. You like?” Feb spun around to model, then put her hand on Kelly’s chest. “Sweetie, meet my little sister-slash-protégé, Flan.”

“Nice to meet you, Flan,” the haute bush hunter boyfriend said. “And yes, before you ask, it’s supposed to be ironic.”

I smiled at Feb. “I like him already. Where’s Patch? I thought I just heard his voice.”

Feb rolled her eyes and flung open the door to the coat closet under the stairs. A huddle of bodies, one of which I recognized as that of my older brother, Patch, tumbled out in a lump.

“Remember when we used to wrap fruit roll-ups around our fingers and lick them off?” Feb muttered to me under her breath. I nodded, not sure where she was going with the question. “I think Patch’s new girlfriend has him confused with a fruit roll-up.”

I looked at Patch, who was bright red at having been busted making out in the coatroom. He did have a strange girl attached to his neck, but something else was different about him too. He was wearing a fitted yellow button-down and gray pin-striped slacks. I almost didn’t recognize my vintage-T-shirt-only-wearing brother underneath the fancy clothes. Only a girl he really liked could get Patch to dress up for family dinner. At least his hair was still sticking out in all directions—that part I recognized.

Patch pulled away from the girl and gave me a friendly nod. "Hey sis. How ya been? This is Agnes." He sounded out of breath.

Agnes smiled at me warmly and said hi, but quickly turned her attention back to Patch. She focused on smoothing his hair out and giggling in his ear.

Feb made a gagging motion as my dad's voice called out from the kitchen.

"Mom's threatening to eat all the spring rolls if you kids don't get in here."

As the five of us headed into the dining room for dinner, Feb took me by the arm and pulled me back. She gestured at Patch and Agnes. "Never, I repeat *never* rent a houseboat off Capri for a week with those two."

"Why?" I said, wishing I wasn't always in school to miss the fun sibling bonding trips that Patch and Feb took every month. "That sounds so fun."

"Fun would require your brother to keep his hands off Hag-nes for more than three minutes at a time," Feb corrected.

"Ah, I can see that," I admitted, "but double-dating must be fun. Do you go on double dates with your other friends? Have they all met Kelly?"

Feb looked thoughtful for a minute. "To tell you the truth, Flan, since I started dating Kelly, I haven't really seen much of my friends."

Huh? But Feb had always been my friendship role model. She was legendary for her elaborate social circles. She had more friends on Facebook than anyone I knew!

"But what about Jade Moodswing?" I asked, remembering how tight they'd been at the French designer's fashion show just last month. "Or Opal Jagger?"

"I dunno." She shrugged. "We've sort of just . . . drifted apart. Nothing dramatic. You'll see when you get serious with someone. It's just one of those things."

I looked at my sister, who was back to giggling with Kelly. I had always looked up to her, but at that moment I found myself hoping I *didn't* end up like her. No matter how great things were with Alex, I never wanted to drift apart from my friends. It just felt so sad. There must be a way to strike a balance, right?

Trying to put her words out of my mind, I headed for my usual seat next to Patch. But Agnes—not surprisingly—had slid in before me.

"Hey Flan," Kelly said, pointing to a seat between himself and Feb. "Sit here."

"Everyone settled?" my dad asked. "Let's grub."

While he distributed chopsticks, the rest of us got to work opening up the stacks of steaming white boxes of food.

"No Alex tonight, Flan?" my mother asked. She'd changed into a black and white silk kimono and laced her chopsticks through her hair. "He's such a hunk, isn't he?"

"He's having dinner with his grandmother," I said, slurping a bowl of egg drop wonton soup.

"Awwww," everyone at the table seemed to say at once.

I looked up at them. "What?"

"That's too bad," my father said.

"Really sucks," Patch agreed.

"Would have loved to meet him," Kelly said.

"I'm sorry, Flan," my mother said, sounding like she'd taken empathy lessons from SBB.

"It's no big deal." I shrugged. "I saw him yesterday." I mean, it would have been great to have Alex there, but it wasn't like I couldn't function without him. Right?

"I'm just glad to be with you guys," I said, convincing myself.

"That's nice," my mother said. "Isn't that nice, dear?" she asked my father. When he smiled at her across the table, it was hard not to notice the silent closeness between them—between all the couples.

But then, midbite of her scallion pancake, my mother hopped up from the table. "I completely forgot to call Gloria about our donation to the Guggenheim's restructuring. BRB!"

As my siblings and I groaned at Mom's perpetual overuse of out-of-date slang, my dad sighed and picked up his BlackBerry. "Well, if your mother has permission to do business at the dinner table, I'm just going to send one quick e-mail."

I looked to Patch, who usually harassed my parents when they got bogged down by work during family time, but he was consumed—literally—by Agnes, who still seemed to have her lips attached to his neck.

Geez, if I was looking to my family for examples on how to be in a relationship, this dinner party was leaving me a little uninspired. I turned to Feb and Kelly, the last couple standing.

"So," I asked, trying to make normal conversation. "You guys have been traveling in the bush? Is it hot there or what?"

"Not really. It cools down at night," Kelly said.

"Are you kidding? It's been like living in a sauna," Feb said, oddly riled up. "And you never let us use the air conditioner! You wonder why I always have to wear my hair up!"

"We've been over this," Kelly said, shaking his head. "I think you know the carbon footprint of the average air-conditioning-using American."

Whoa, who knew I could hit such a sore spot by asking the most boring question in the world? If Kelly and Feb were fighting over the weather, how did they handle the hard stuff?

To diffuse the tension, I picked up the first tub of food in front of me. "More beef and broccoli, anyone?"

Feb looked at the food and then at Kelly with narrow eyes. "No thanks, Flan," she hissed. "We're *vegan* now."

"Oh, just lay on the guilt," Kelly moaned. "Everything is all my fault!"

A squeaky smooching sound—the parting of lips across the table—put a pause in their argument. Agnes was taking a breather from Patch and had turned to face us. "Could you guys keep it down over there?"

"Yeah," Patch agreed. "You're sort of harshing our mellow."

"That's it," my mother reappeared from the kitchen. "None of the brainiacs in the art world know how to read a simple e-mail. I have to dash uptown to straighten out this mess." She paused and looked around the table. "I'm so sorry to have ruined this lovely dinner. We'll reschedule, okay? And next time, Flan, you must make sure your partner can join us! You know what they say—nothing makes a mother hen happier than seeing all her chicks settled down. . . ."

Everyone around me seemed to take a cue from my mom and started stacking up the plates. Before I knew it, I was alone in the dining room. So much for a fun family dinner.

I was used to being alone at the dinner table, but I wasn't used to being alone when the rest of my family was *home*. I couldn't remember the last time I'd actually ended a family dinner feeling worse than before it. Was it because everyone was partnered off tonight except me? Or was it just because I hadn't had my fortune cookie?

Making jokes out of the cheesy Chin-Chin fortunes was usually our favorite part of the meal. I reached for the bag and pulled out one of the cookies.

I popped open the wrapping and performed my superstitious ritual of eating the whole cookie with my eyes closed before I unfolded the fortune. In a weird way, it felt like a lot was riding on this moment. Maybe if my family couldn't offer me relationship

Chapter 4

THREE SCOOPS, TWO SPOONS, ONE SHOCKER

An hour later, there was a knock on my door. Wondering if it would be the four-eyed, kissing Pagnes monster, or maybe Feb in tears after a blowout with Kelly, or possibly one of my parents checking in on my lonely evening, I opened up the door.

"Guess who?" Alex was standing in the hall outside my bedroom wearing his Hermès navy peacoat and a big grin.

"What are you doing here?" I asked.

"Kidnapping you," he said. "Come on."

I glanced back at the chemistry notebook on my bed, and took it as a sign that Noodles had crawled on top of it and fallen asleep. "I'll grab my coat," I said.

Outside my brownstone, Alex's driver was waiting in a town car. He opened the door for me and I slid in.

"Where are we going?" I asked—praying for

Scoops, my favorite ice cream store in the city. But then, we wouldn't need the driver to go to Scoops. It was just down the block on Bleecker Street. . . .

"You'll see," Alex said, raising an eyebrow.

The car hurtled south, through the West Village and into Chinatown, before taking a left on Canal Street. The streets were damp with slushy rain, and red and gold flags hung from storefronts, announcing the Chinese New Year. Even through the windows, the air was heavy with the scent of seafood shops lining Canal.

When the car pulled to a stop on a quiet street below Canal, Alex said, "I felt bad about missing Chinese food with your family, so I thought I'd make it up to you with Chinese dessert."

Ooh, he was good. He was very good.

"You mentioned once that you were on a quest for the best mocha chip ice cream in the city," Alex continued. "I know you think you've found it at Scoops, but you'd be cheating yourself if you didn't try this version."

We stepped off the damp street into the old-fashioned ice cream shop, loud with a surprisingly large crowd. All the flavors were written in Chinese on a huge whiteboard. I stood on tiptoe to kiss Alex on the lips. "This is so cool and authentic," I said. "I love it."

When I first met Alex, I thought he was your typical, partying bad boy. He wore designer motorcycle boots and played punk rock gigs at Hamptons parties. At first, I was impressed by the way he didn't care about the social rules that everyone else in our scene was so obsessed with—oh, and I was also super attracted to him. But mostly, I was intimidated.

But ever since our first date at Wollman Rink last month, I'd realized that for every thing about Alex that might paint him as a certain type of guy, he broke the rule by also being something completely opposite. Like, he wasn't just the captain of the Dalton lacrosse team—he was also an alternate on the math team. And his goal in life was to become a screenwriter, even though his dad assumed he'd go to law school and take over the family firm. And there was a really good chance he'd do all of those things. By now I knew that I should never assume I knew everything about Alex, because he always had a surprise up his sleeve. Kinda like how I shouldn't have assumed I knew all the good ice cream places in the city. . . .

Alex took care of ordering and handed me the bowl with tidy scoops of mocha chocolate chip. I grinned and took a bite.

"Omigod," I said with my mouth full of perfectly soft ice cream. "Scoops just got some serious competition."

"Save room," he said, snagging a spoonful. "This is not the last stop."

I took my to-go cup and followed Alex back to the car, excited to see what else he had planned.

"So how was dinner?" he said as we continued west along Canal Street. "What'd I miss?"

I thought about divulging how crazy my siblings were acting over their new S.O.'s but I didn't want to scare my still-new boyfriend, so I just said, "Oh, you know, the usual. Mom dressed in theme; Dad oversaw the passing of food; kids fought over the extra fortune cookie."

"I'm sorry I missed it," Alex said before telling the driver to take the Brooklyn Bridge. "I hope you got your hands on that last cookie."

As we drove over the bridge, taking in arguably the very best view of the glittery city, I thought back to my lonely moment at the dining room table. "Yeah," I said. "I guess I did."

"And?" Alex prompted. "What'd the fortune say?"

I laughed and started blushing for no reason. "It said, 'Have a wonderful night.' "

"Well," Alex said, as we stepped out of the car for the second time, on an equally dark street corner in Dumbo, "no one can say we didn't try."

The Brooklyn Ice Cream Company is legendary

for its no-frills flavors and amazing ingredients. It used to be a favorite of mine, but I realized I hadn't been back here since I was a kid—and I'd definitely never tried their mocha chocolate chip.

Alex and I strolled along the promenade and sampled the second contender's ice cream. "Hmm . . . It is chocolatier," I said thoughtfully. "And meltier . . . Hard to pick a favorite!"

"Don't pick a favorite yet," Alex said, steering me back toward the moonlit car. "If you think you can handle it, I've got one more place for us to hit."

"I think you underestimate my ice cream–eating capabilities," I joked.

We crossed the bridge back into the hustle of Manhattan and headed north again toward SoHo.

"This next place isn't technically ice cream—but the mocha chocolate chip is good enough that I think we should make an allowance."

"Ooh, I think I know where we're going," I squealed when the car stopped on Spring Street. We got out in front of the neon circular sign of Rice to Riches, a funny little café that serves dozens of crazy flavors of rice pudding.

By then, I was getting pretty full, so we decided to walk off all the mocha chocolate chip with a stroll around the neighborhood. Alex had his arm around me and I fed him spoonfuls of rice pudding—and only occasionally wondered whether this type of PDA would make Feb roll her eyes and vow not to rent a houseboat with Alex and me. I'd gotten as far as picturing the six of us, all hanging out on a boat for a week of island-hopping in the Mediterranean, when Alex came to a sudden halt.

"Look who it is," I heard a guy's voice say and looked up to see Alex's friends from Dalton—Remy Wise, Troy Fishman, and Xander. I thought Camille had said this morning that she and Xander had a study date tonight. . . .

"Oh, hey guys," Alex said.

"Hey Alex," Troy said, a twinge of annoyance on his face. "You know, your grandmother looks an awful lot like your girlfriend."

"Yeah," Remy said, crossing his arms. "You say you're having dinner with Grandma and then ditch us for Flan? Nice."

Alex looked flustered and shook his head. "Guys, I didn't ditch you. I *did* have dinner with my grandmother. I just picked Flan up a little while ago. What's the big deal?"

It didn't make any sense that the guys would think Alex ditched them. Had I done something to make them so cold?

"Whatever, man," Xander said, barely looking at me. "Seems like you're busy, or whatever."

Why was this black cloud hanging over the group? And why was it so easy for me to imagine this exact scene happening between me and *my* friends?

Alex looked stressed. He was running his hands through his hair. I put my hand on his arm. "Hey," I whispered, "I hope you didn't feel guilted into hanging out with me tonight. I didn't mean to—"

"No," he said quickly. "I wanted to hang out with you. I definitely didn't expect to piss anyone off by hanging out with you." He looked up at Xander. "Just because Camille . . ." He trailed off.

"Just because Camille what?" I asked. "Xander, where's Camille?"

Troy scoffed. "Like you don't know, Flan."

Xander was looking at his feet.

"Know what?" I asked. "What's going on?"

"I figured she would have told you," Xander admitted finally. "We broke up. A few hours ago."

I looked down at the remaining rice pudding in my bowl, which looked anything but appetizing. Alex's friends were all pissed at him for hanging out with me. Now Alex was squirming and clearly weirded out about missing post-breakup dude time. Worst of all, my best friend was probably sitting at home alone, heartbroken and miserable. And right before Valentine's Day! Poor Camille.

And did this mean I was now the only one in my circle of friends to have a boyfriend? That definitely wasn't going to make my balancing act any easier.

Chapter 5
A LATTE WITH A SHOT OF ATTITUDE

The next morning, I set my alarm forty-five minutes early so I could be dressed and ready to hang with Morgan before school. We were meeting at Agata & Valentino's café on Seventy-ninth Street, and I didn't want to be late.

Ever since I'd enrolled at Thoney in January, Morgan had been a funny, comforting presence in my life. In fact, she'd been the very first person to be nice to me when I showed up shaking in my Moschino all-weather boots as a Thoney infant. I remember how nervous I was, not knowing how to get anywhere in the unfamiliar building. If it hadn't been for Morgan's peppy fashion compliment, I might still be frozen in the marble Thoney foyer.

My first month at school had kind of been a trial by fire—complete with an all-out election war over Thoney's coveted Virgil coordinator with Kennedy

Pearson and Willa Rubenstein (longtime frenemy and newfound enemy, respectively). But now that I was happily comfortable in my school life, I knew that I owed a big chunk of that happiness to my friendship with Morgan. Recently, though, I could tell she'd been kind of down. Last month, she'd gone on two dates with a random Exeter boy, only to hear that he'd been seen making out with a sophomore at a party three days later. None of our friends had even known she liked him that much, but there had definitely been a downward shift in the fun rating of the music she downloaded to her iPod.

For the past two weeks, she'd seemed to be actively trying to burst her eardrums with gloomy Cat Power music. I knew that her bubbly, indie rock–loving former self would be ashamed at some of her current musical choices, so recently, I'd been brainstorming ways to get the old Morgan back in business. I'd been meaning to plan something really fun for the two of us to do together over the weekend.

But now it was another Monday morning. How had a whole two days passed with us barely speaking? Morgan *had* been at her family house upstate on Friday night, and I *had* been with Alex on Saturday . . . and Sunday.

But this week I was determined to focus on our friendship.

I stepped into the newly revamped café of Agata & Valentino. It used to be just your run-of-the-mill gourmet grocery store. My mom and I would swing by for rotisserie chicken and grape gazpacho after she picked me up at my grade school, Miss Mallard's. But last year, the owners expanded the store to double its former size. Now there were a chic little coffee bar and pastry shop on the opposite corner from the grocery store. The place was always a little hectic with stroller pushing mothers and UES museum curators, but it was still the best spot in the neighborhood for a pick-me-up before school.

When I found Morgan in her gray Vera Wang toggle coat, she was waiting at the head of the line for her soy latte with hazelnut syrup.

"Morning, sunshine," I said, tapping her on the shoulder.

She turned and gave me her usual air-kiss, but she looked unusually tired.

"I'll believe the sunshine bit when I see it," she said, gesturing outside at the dismal gray February morning. "Can we make that a double shot in my latte?" she shouted over at the barista.

"I brought you something," I sang cheerily, holding up a new Vampire Weekend LP Patch had brought back from L.A.

"Oh," she said flatly, eyeing the CD. "Thanks, Flan."

"But you love Vampire Weekend," I said. "And this is an unreleased live album. Where's my frantic I-love-you-Flan jig?"

"God, that espresso maker's loud," Morgan said, clutching her temples. "Is it, like, insanely loud in here? Let's go outside. I can't hear anything."

I glanced at the terrace, where the iced-over patio furniture looked pretty forlorn.

"I guess we can just head toward school?" I said, kind of disappointed not to have a relaxing catch-up convo in the café. Instead, we grabbed our drinks and made for the door pronto.

"Sure." Morgan shrugged. "School. Where we'll be greeted by poster after poster after poster trying to sell us on how 'wild' and 'amazing' the Valentine's Day Dance is going to be."

Whoa. Someone had woken up as bitter as the unsweetened espresso I was drinking.

"Come on, Morg," I said. "Who cares what the lame student council posters claim? If we want the Valentine's Day Dance to be fun, all we have to do is show up and *make* it fun. Tell me you haven't lost faith in our powers of partying? Now, on to the important stuff," I said, tugging on her coat playfully. "What are you going to wear? You're the only one in our crew who looks good in red, so I nominate you to wear the bold and dramatic color of Cupid."

Morgan looked at me like I'd just asked her what she was going to wear to her beheading.

"You're joking, right, Flan? I thought we'd all agreed on this. None of us are going to that lame dance. Sadie Hawkins? For Valentine's Day? I mean, whose idea was that? Probably the dean's—the *male* dean."

"Morgan," I said, putting my arm around her as we turned onto East Eighty-eighth Street. "We're an all-girls school. If we don't ask the dates to our own dance, how are they supposed to know about it?"

"That's not the point," she huffed. "The point is—"

Uh-oh, Morgan's Random Exeter Boy baggage was rearing its ugly head again.

"The point is . . ." she repeated, unwinding her red Colette scarf from around her neck. Her face was flushed. ". . . that Camille has just been dumped by another typical jerky guy. We have to boycott the dance to show solidarity for our friend, and our gender as a whole."

Oh. Shoot! I could not believe I'd forgotten about Camille and Xander. I mean, I hadn't really forgotten—after Alex dropped me off last night, I'd only called and texted her about eleven times. Her mood online was still set to romantic—so obviously she wasn't ready to let the world know about her breakup just yet. I figured that maybe she just wanted a little time, that maybe she'd come to me when she was ready.

But Morgan seemed to know the gory details. Obviously, I was missing something. And had she kind of spat out those last words a little bit more viciously than necessary?

"Okay," I said, digging through my bag for my Chanel Tulip lip gloss so Morgan couldn't see the look of embarrassment on my face. "I guess I missed that conference call about the dance." I shrugged. "If you guys don't want to go for Camille's sake, of course I'll boycott with you."

But even as I said the words, I knew I wasn't hiding my disappointment very well. As we stepped into Thoney and walked through the entryway hall, Morgan swung by her locker. For the first time, I noticed all the posters that she'd had been talking about:

COME TO THE CUPID COTILLION!

TAKE ACTION—DON'T LET YOUR DATE GET SCOOPED UP BY ANOTHER WOMAN!

ROSES ARE RED, VIOLETS ARE BLUE, EVERYONE WILL BE AT THE V-DAY DANCE—WILL YOU?

So they were a little dorky. The thing was, I *did* want to go to the Valentine's Dance. It had never occurred to me not to go.

Just then, Willa Rubenstein, class president and resident sociopath, brushed by in a swishy candy apple red Moschino skirt.

"Aww, cute," she said in her patented saccharine voice. "Cinderella wants to go to the ball. Too bad rumor has it none of your posse can get dates. Planning the cover-up girl-power night instead, I hope."

Before I could respond, Morgan squeezed my shoulder. Willa gave her coat a scrutinizing glare and swished away.

"I knew you wouldn't ditch us for some stupid dance just because you have a boyfriend," Morgan said, oblivious to Willa. "But it's gonna take more than a dance boycott to help Camille. You know how much of a wreck she is right now."

I did? Maybe I would know if Camille had returned any of my calls last night. Morgan had been so quick to point out the fact that I had a boyfriend. That couldn't have anything to do with Camille's silence, could it?

Morgan continued, looking more energized than she had all morning. "We'll have to do triage pretty much constantly until Camille is feeling better. Which is why we're scheduling an emergency cheer-up girl-fest today after school."

"We are?"

"Of course," Morgan said, looking at me like I was crazy not to recognize the need for immediate breakup triage.

"Of course," I echoed. We were standing in the hallway where we'd part ways when the first bell rang in a few minutes. Morgan would go to her Latin class and I'd go to AP French—but somehow, it seemed like we were already speaking different languages.

"So what's the plan?" I asked.

"After last period, we're meeting at the Bliss uptown. Harper scheduled group seaweed facials and body wraps. No boys allowed."

The thought of any guy actually wanting to witness five girls looking like monsters under a full body coating of green seaweed almost made me laugh, but when I looked at Morgan she was all boy-boycotting business.

"Got it." I nodded. "No boys."

As Morgan and I air-kissed good-bye, I thought I could sense a renewed purpose in her that I hadn't seen in weeks. It was great of her to take charge of Operation Heal Camille, but it felt a little like Morgan was *looking* for an excuse to drum up boy-hatred. Of course, I'd do whatever it took to be there for my friends, but I didn't think that needed to include swearing off all boys altogether.

Just before I stepped into my French class, I reached for my phone to put it on silent. While Morgan was telling me the details of our girls-only spa trip tonight, I'd missed a couple texts from Alex:

WE STILL ON FOR KOREAN BBQ IN MY HOOD TONIGHT?

Then:

HOPE YOU LIKE IT SPICY.

Double shoot. Would I ever stop constantly overbooking myself? Ugh. Alex had been talking up this Korean BBQ restaurant all week, and I really wanted to go. But . . . my best friend needed me. And it seemed like my other friends needed me to be there for her, too.

I wasn't exactly sure how spicy I liked my Korean BBQ, but I did know that if I wanted to keep the heat off myself in my social circle, I had only one choice.

How did you say "rain check" in Korean?

Chapter 6

UNDER COVER . . . OR OVER THE TOP?

Sandwiched in the lunch line between my pals Harper Alden and Amory Wilx, I got a taste of just how widespread the anti-boy syndrome had become.

"I mean, Camille *trusted* Xander," Harper was saying as she readjusted her massive black Ralph Lauren sunglasses to hold back her straight golden locks. "And the way he just dropped her like that—it's completely disrespectful to her as a *woman*."

I loved Harper, but in some ways she was pretty traditional. Everything in her life had a mannered, high-society quality to it. I turned to Amory, who'd grown up with Harper and almost always called her out on her antiquated views of dating.

But Amory was nodding her head so enthusiastically, I thought her Candace Ang hoops might fall out of her ears.

"I know," she said, selecting a fruit salad from the

line. "It's like boys only want us on *their* schedules. They're are so capricious, just picking and choosing whatever girl, whenever they feel like it. Why should it be up to them all the time?"

I laughed and pointed at her fruit salad. "So says the girl who picks all the kiwi off one fruit salad and tosses it back with just cantaloupe left."

"Not the same thing!" Amory insisted, but she laughed. "Okay, maybe that was a little ruthless."

"This is why people shouldn't jump into relationships," Harper continued on her tirade. "My parents have a strict rule: no new guy can take me out until he has enough manners to show up at our house and introduce himself to my father."

"Geez," I joked, grabbing a bottle of iced jasmine tea. "If I had to wait around for my dad to be home to meet my new boyfriends, I'd never get a date!"

"That's not true, Flan," Amory said. "Alex has met your parents, hasn't he?"

"Briefly." I grinned, remember my mom talking about what a hunk he was at dinner last night. "He's pret-ty *amaz*—"

I froze midgush. Both Harper and Amory were staring at me as if I were praising my new pet tarantula. Whoops, better change the subject fast.

"Have we actually gotten Camille's side of this

story?" I asked as we paid for our grub. Both Harper and Amory looked at each other and shrugged. "I mean, so far, what we know about the breakup of the century is only conjecture, isn't it? Where *is* Camille, anyway?"

What if it wasn't that bad? What if, on her anti-boy rampage, Morgan had blown the story just slightly out of proportion? What if there was still a chance to hit pause on the man-hating DVD all my friends seemed to be tuning into? Maybe, just maybe, there was a way to turn things around in time for us to rock the Valentine's Dance like we had Virgil. . . .

Suddenly, Amory pointed dramatically.

"There," she gasped, breathless.

I followed Amory's finger toward the fourth table from the door, our daily lunch spot. Hunched over the table alone in her black Burberry trench was the shadow of my best friend. At that moment, Camille looked up to give us a full view of her tear-streaked face. We were on the other side of the cafeteria, but even if we'd been standing right in front of her, she still wouldn't have seen us. Her eyes were completely glazed over in misery.

"She needs us," Harper said, starting toward her. But before she'd even taken three steps, she turned back around to me. "And Flan, for Camille's sake, try to zip it on the Alex stories for like twenty minutes, okay?"

I blanched. That seemed a little uncalled for! But we were supposed to be uniting to focus on Camille, so I brushed off the harshness and just nodded.

As I followed the other girls toward the table, trying to imagine how things between Camille and Xander had fallen apart so quickly, I felt a sudden yank on my right elbow. I turned around to find the most un-Thoney-looking girl I'd ever seen within these walls.

She had bright red hair pulled into a high side ponytail and tied with a yellow ribbon. She was wearing a purple gingham shirt tied in a knot at her waist, and her face was dotted with a smattering of auburn freckles. Wait a minute—those freckles looked abnormally large and didn't exactly match her coloring. And underneath that thick mop of hair, I could have sworn I recognized . . .

A look of terror crossed the girl's face, and before I could say anything she clapped her hand over my mouth and dragged me—and my precariously balanced bowl of vegetarian pho—behind the vending machines.

"Don't make a sound," she hissed once we were alone. As soon as she uttered the words, I knew my suspicions had been right.

"SBB," I said, "*what* are you doing here? And *what* are you wearing?"

"I texted you an hour ago to see if it was okay if I came for . . ." She paused. ". . . a visit."

"I've been in chem lab all morning," I said, taking in her pleated jeans and old-school Keds. "And for the record, in the past, *a visit* means you stopping by with sushi and a cute bag you just picked up at Barneys. What's up with the gingham? I mean, I know urban cowgirl was in a couple seasons ago, but this seems like a stretch."

SBB sighed and collapsed pretzel-style on the parquet floor. "I know," she heaved. "I'm hideous. I just . . . I didn't want to be recognized on my first day of school! My audition for *Blinker High* is right around the corner. I know you said you'd help me unlock the mystery of high school, but I was just sitting around in my underwater pilates class this morning, feeling like every second that I didn't spend preparing for this part was a waste of time. I got so distracted, I almost drowned, Flannie! So I figured—I figured I'd enroll at Thoney with the very most wonderful high school student in the whole world." She looked up to gauge my reaction. "Just, you know, for a little while."

"Oh, SBB," I said, joining her on the floor and putting my arms around her. This audition clearly meant a lot to her. "Well . . . welcome to Thoney. I'm Flan and I'll be your tour guide through the treacherous world of high school." I tugged on her braid. "Lesson one: you don't have to dress like a complete geek—no offense—to avoid being recognized as your movie-star self."

"I don't?" she asked, wide-eyed.

"Uh-uh. Maybe start with a slightly less offensive wig and see how it goes?" I suggested. I slid the bowl of pho in between us and offered SBB first shot at the chopsticks.

"Wow, you have Vietnamese food in your cafeteria?" she asked, slurping up some of the spicy noodles. "This is *good.* I thought it was all Tater Tots and Jell-O."

"Lesson two." I held up two fingers. "Thoney is not your normal high school."

"Should I be taking notes?" SBB asked. "I've seen some girls walking around with *really* cute planners. I could get a planner like yours." She reached for my new Kate Spade notebook. It was flipped open to this afternoon, where I'd written: *Man-hating spa treatment with the girls.*

I sneaked a peek around the vending machines at my other friends. I knew I needed to be there for

Camille, but at least for now, the other girls seemed to have her tears under control. I didn't want to abandon SBB before she felt settled at Thoney.

"What's this?" SBB asked, pointing at today's box in my planner. "Does Thoney have an after-school spa club? Or are Bliss trips exclusive to Thoney too?"

"I dunno," I said. "I think boy trouble is pretty universal to high school girls. Although maybe not everyone does therapy via seaweed wraps . . ."

"Oh no," SBB said, snapping shut my planner. "Don't tell me something's wrong with you and Alex?"

"Far from it," I said, glad to be able to admit that. "It's Camille. She and Xander split up yesterday."

Before I knew it, I had spilled the whole story to SBB—from my early morning coffee and complaining session with Morgan, to my convo in line with Amory and Harper, to the sad sight of one very heartbroken Camille across the cafeteria, to the final realization that all of my friends wanted to boycott the first dance I'd every actually been excited about.

"But you *must* go to the Valentine's Dance, Flan," SBB said. "Think about how great you and Alex will look together all dressed up!"

"I know, but it won't be any fun if all my other friends bail," I said. I sneaked a glance around the vending machines to check in on Camille. She was dabbing her eyes with her handkerchief and Morgan was standing up, red-faced and waving her finger in the air—clear signs of an anti-boy tirade in progress. Making it to the Valentine's Day dance didn't look good.

"Flan," SBB said, looking at me like I was missing a really obvious solution to my problem, "how many times have you seen my movie *Heartbreak Hotel*?"

"Only about three hundred." I laughed, remembering SBB's role in last summer's smash hit about an eccentric millionaire living in the Beverly Hills Hotel. "You made me read Ronny Pepp's lines opposite you for a month before shooting started, remember?"

SBB nodded. "You do a really great Ronny Pepp," she recalled. "And you must also remember the brilliant idea that my character came up with when all her friends were heartbroken. . . ."

Simultaneously, SBB and I exclaimed: "She fixed them all up with dates!"

"Exactly," SBB said, looking proud of herself. "Look, you know a ton of guys. And all your friends are megacatches. I'm sure you could fix them up with Valentine's Day Dance–worthy dates in no time." SBB put her hand to her chest like she was about to make a grand confession. "I may not know high school—*yet!*—but I do know about matters of the heart. Trust me, all it would take to turn your crew around is a little bit of matchmaking."

I nodded. "You're so right," I said. "None of them would be anti-boy if I could find them the right boys! Flan the matchmaker. Why didn't I think of that?"

Feeling immediately more empowered about the fate of my Valentine's Day, I sneaked a final peek at my pals across the lunchroom. Everyone had stood up to recycle their trash—everyone except Camille, whose head was back in her hands in her Hunchback of Thoney pose. Hmmm. Finding a match for Camille should probably be my first priority.

"Flannie?" SBB asked innocently. "You're not going to tell anyone who I am, are you? I won't be able to really immerse myself if I know that my disguise isn't airtight. My Jakey-pie told me that I need to try to lose myself in my role while I'm here." She grasped my hands tightly. "You'll help me be a real live high school girl, won't you?"

Even as my mind was scrolling through all of the guys I knew, I had to laugh at SBB's earnestness.

"Don't worry, Not-SBB. Your crazy secret is safe with me."

Chapter 7

THE SEAWEED SESSIONS

A few hours later, I was terry-cloth robe–clad and lounging in the ladies' waiting room at Bliss spa on Forty-ninth Street. Around me, Harper, Amory, Morgan, and Camille flipped through fashion magazines and munched on platters of olives, cucumbers, spicy hummus, and apple wedges. Usually, I loved this pre-spa treatment ritual at Bliss, but today I was consumed by the fact that I still hadn't gotten a chance to check in on Camille about how she was handling the breakup.

Across the room, I caught her eye. "Whoops," I said, looking down at my wrist. "Just realized I forgot to take off my watch." I cocked my head toward the locker room while holding Camille's eyes. "I'll just go throw it in my locker so it doesn't get all seaweed-wrapped."

"Me too," Camille said, stuffing her wrist in her

pocket to hide the fact that she'd already taken off her watch. "I'll go with you."

Once we were out of earshot of the other girls, I gave Camille a big, silent hug.

"Where've you been all day?" she asked, her voice breaking slightly. "I looked for you at lunch."

"I . . . uh . . ." I stalled, remembering SBB's plea for secrecy, even from Camille. "I realized I had to help Ms. Demsey with the layout for the newsletter. But I've wanted to talk to you all day. Everyone kept saying how bummed you've been, and after I saw Xander last night, I tried to call you, but—"

"Wait, you saw Xander last night?" Her forehead wrinkled and she bit her lip. "Why didn't you tell me?"

"I tried to call you all night," I said, putting my hand on her arm. "When I didn't hear from you, I figured you weren't up for talking. For what it's worth, Xander looked pretty upset about it."

"Good, I hope he looks upset." Camille crossed her arms, getting the giant sleeves of the terry-cloth robe tangled up in each other. "No, I don't. Yes, I do. I don't know, Flan. I've never been so confused."

"What happened with you guys?" I asked, helping to untangle Camille from her robe. "Everything seemed so good."

Camille nodded and sniffed. "He said it was *too*

good. He said he got scared. Does that sound like the biggest lie you've ever heard or what?"

I was about to say no, that in a way I understood what it felt like to be nervous about feeling so strongly about someone, but when I saw the fire in Camille's eyes, I knew that wasn't what she wanted to hear.

"I refuse to mope around forever," she huffed. "And I will *not* be one of those bitter girls who sits around on Valentine's Day, crying into a box of tissues, watching Lifetime movies and eating Lindt's."

The image of film-snob Camille watching Lifetime movies made both of us laugh.

"I need to snap out of this funk before you guys start thinking of me as your downer friend," she said, as if she were convincing herself.

"Camille," I said, tossing my watch in my bag and snapping my locker shut again, "I know you pride yourself on being the world's most positive person—and I love that about you. But this breakup just happened yesterday. You might need to give yourself a little time to feel it."

As soon as I said the words, I realized that completely went against the plan SBB had helped me hatch about getting my friends hooked up with new guys for the Valentine's Dance, but it felt like the right thing to say. Camille was going through something heavy. It might have to be up to her to decide when she was ready to move on. I realized then that if she needed me to skip the Valentine's Day Dance, I'd do it without question.

"Hey girls." Amory stuck her head into the locker room. With a grin, she attempted her Swedish masseuse impersonation, sticking out her chest, batting her eyes, and raising her voice intonations an octave. "They're ready for our treatment!"

We all cracked up. When I first met Amory, I was drawn to her funky style and effortless poise. Now what I loved the most about her was what a huge goofball she could be. She could always come up with something to lighten the mood.

"And," she continued, shimmying her shoulders, "guess who's working today?"

"Georgio?" Camille and I gasped at the same time. Georgio was an immaculate bronze god masseur from Greece. We hadn't seen him since the last time we'd all fought over which one of us would be the recipient of his magic touch.

Now Amory grinned and raised her eyebrows. "We all agreed to donate him to *you* today, Camille."

"Oh, you guys, I couldn't possibly accept such a gift," Camille said, swatting her hand. "Well, okay, if you insist."

But hey, if my friends wanted to nudge Camille

toward drooling over other guys, I was definitely all for that.

We filed down the tranquil hallway into the lavender candlelit group massage room. Five beds were set up like lotus petals, with all the heads facing one another so we could chat while the spa technicians worked their magic. We all lay down on our stomachs and grinned.

"It's been too long since we've done this," Harper said.

"Waaaay too long," Morgan agreed, closing her eyes. "The last time we were here, they were playing Carrie Underwood on satellite radio."

Leave it to Morgan to categorize time according to what music was in or on its way out.

"Maybe I should get dumped more often," Camille said. "You know, to give us a reason to indulge."

When everyone's face fell, she added, "I'm *kidding*, you guys. I don't want us all to feel like we have to tiptoe around it. Xander broke up with me. Life goes on, right?"

"Right," we all agreed, looking down at our beds.

In a rare moment of chattiness, Georgio leaned down to Camille and said, "Whoever hurt you is an idiot, Princess. A beautiful flower like you should have any man she chooses."

Even in the dimly lit room, I could tell Camille was bright red. But Georgio was right: Camille was a total catch. Maybe what she needed now was a guy who wasn't afraid to remind her of that. It was a shame Georgio wasn't a viable option.

Camille sighed. "Maybe I just need to, you know, put the whole thing out of my mind."

Exactly! I thought. Put Xander out of her mind with the help of an older, more mature, more Georgio-like guy.

"Exactly," Morgan said. "Which is why the rest of us have sworn off boys indefinitely to support you. Right, girls?"

"Right," Harper chimed in evenly, and Amory nodded in agreement.

"Right," I added. Sigh.

I looked up at the other girls to see if I could gauge what they thought of Morgan's guy-ditching doctrine. Harper looked stoic as usual. In fact, something about the way she was lying there, sheet-clad, reminded me of someone. . . .

It struck me out of nowhere. She looked exactly like the subject of a painting in our country house in Connecticut! Patch's artist friend Trevor had painted it last summer when he was studying at Julliard, and my mother thought he was so talented that she'd bought it to hang over our fireplace. I remembered my mother grilling Trevor about his blossoming talent, but when she'd asked him who his muse was, he'd blushed and stammered that he hadn't met her yet. He had just painted his ideal beauty.

I wondered if Trevor was still painting in New York. And I wondered how quickly I could arrange to introduce him to his future muse. . . .

"Flip," my decidedly un-Georgio-like masseuse commanded. I turned over onto my back so the hefty Swedish woman could slather the cool green seaweed mask on my other side.

I closed my eyes and continued to let SBB's matchmaking advice marinate in my thoughts. Where was I? I'd already come up with a type of guy for Camille—now I just had to think of the right older, handsome man for her. And Harper would be totally excited when I told her about my plot to make her an artist's muse. I craned my neck to the side to look at Amory to see if inspiration would strike a third time. She caught my gaze, winked, and stuck out her tongue at me.

Good, now what guy did I know who was as much of a ham as Amory? He would have to have the same stylish exterior and goofball interior—ooh! What about Alex's actor friend, Phil, from the movie premiere? He'd looked pretty amazing in his Kenneth Cole pin-striped suit. And he had been cracking jokes all night. I'd have to ask Alex if he was single. . . .

"Flan? Are you in?" Morgan's voice brought me back to reality.

I looked around the lotus of friends' heads around me. "Of course," I said, without having any idea what I was agreeing to. "Yeah, I'm in."

"Good," Morgan said. "I'll double-check with my parents that our cabin's free next weekend. We'll ski and drink hot chocolate and Jacuzzi and we won't even miss the Valentine's Day Dance at all!"

Wait—what? The Valentine's Day Dance was one thing, but had I just agreed to skip town with the girls the entire Valentine's Day weekend? How was I going to explain that to Alex?

As Morgan went on and on about how much fun we were going to have rejecting boys forever, I could feel my matchmaking plans slipping away from me. And I realized how fast I was going to have to act if I were to have any hope of salvaging the romance of Valentine's Day for my girls—and myself.

Chapter 8
MUSIC TO HER EARS

The next day after school, Morgan and I grabbed a cab and headed to SoHo, to the classy French bistro Balthazar. We were taking a photography class together and had to do a partners photo shoot where the focus was on food. Since Balthazar has some of the most gorgeous (and incredibly delicious) pastries in the universe, we figured there was no better excuse for a field trip.

"Oh my God, I love this song. Can we turn it up?" Morgan asked the cabdriver on the way downtown. She turned to me. "They never play the Kinks on the radio, can you believe this?" She grinned, singing along to the funky rock music.

I nodded in agreement, even though most of the time Morgan's music references were sort of over my head.

"My parent's have the best Kinks vinyl collection

at our cabin," she said. "I'll have to play some for you when we go up there next weekend."

"About next weekend," I started to say. I knew I had to come clean to Morgan that I wasn't as gung-ho as she was about abandoning Valentine's Day, but I wasn't sure how to bring it up.

"Oh, here we are!" Morgan told the cabdriver as we paused on Spring Street to pay the fare. "Let's just hope Balthazar has enough taste to spare us the Valentine overload."

"A romantic French café?" I joked. "That's likely."

Inside the restaurant, the red leather banquettes were packed with cappuccino-sipping power-lunchers, miniature poodles tucked into handbags, and a few saliva-swapping newlyweds. I thought the Valentine's decorations hanging from the ceiling were totally tasteful, but Morgan looked at me and made a gagging motion with her finger.

We decided to eat before we worked, and slid into a booth as far away from the Cupid's arrows and groping couples as possible.

Morgan had just ordered a palmier and a latte, and I was looking forward to my linzertorte and Earl Grey tea, when I felt a strong hand grip my knee under the table.

"Flan, OMG." Morgan's face was white. "*Random Exeter Boy* is over there."

She pointed at a couple two tables down, though I could barely see the guy because his face was being swallowed by a waif girl with dyed red hair. I'd actually never had a chance to meet Random Exeter Boy back during his short-lived romance with Morgan, so I didn't know what to expect. I did know that Morgan was way cuter than the girl he was with today. I looked at Morgan to see how she was taking it, and to my surprise, the color seemed to be coming *back* into her cheeks.

"Hey." I grabbed her hand under the table. "How you doing? Do you want to leave?"

"You know what," she said. "I never liked the way he parted his hair. And look at how he kisses. It's all wrong. Yuck. He hated the Kinks too, if you can believe that! Plus, he does this really weird impersonation of his pet turtle that I just don't think I could ever be cool with."

"I'm gonna need a visual on that," I said.

Morgan scrunched up her lips and retracted her head back into her neck and started speaking in this really slow, hilarious, if-turtles-could-talk voice.

I started cracking up, and when Morgan saw my face, she started laughing too. By the time the waitress arrived with our snacks, we were practically rolling out of the booth.

"So yeah, enough said." I laughed, raising my mug of tea to cheers Morgan. "Looks like it's a good thing Random Exeter Boy didn't exactly come out of his shell. You should never be with someone who doesn't appreciate the Kinks."

When Morgan finally stopped laughing, she sighed. "You know, in a city this big, sometimes I think it really is fate when you run into someone you've been avoiding. Here I've been beating myself up for weeks imagining Random Exeter making out with someone else. Now that I've seen it up close, I'm so not worried about what I'm missing."

"Good," I said, offering her a bite of my linzertorte—and instead of disdaining the heart-shaped, red jelly–filled cookie, she took it.

"This is amazing," she said, wide-eyed. "I can't believe I've never tried one of these before."

"Wait—hold that pose," I said, pulling out the battered old camera I'd gotten for my birthday in sixth grade. "I think this could be just the look I've been trying to get." As Camille posed for delicate bites of the most Valentine's-y of cookies, I took almost a whole roll of film. With all the votives on the tables and the dusk outside, the lighting was perfect, and even more noticeably, something in Morgan's face looked lighter than it had just minutes before. I wondered if now was the right time to bring up the dance.

"Morgan," I said hesitantly, "I know we all agreed to go to your cabin next weekend, and it sounds really great, but—"

"But you want to go to the Valentine's Dance with Alex," she filled in. I nodded. "I know," she said. "I thought about that last night. Maybe I was a little too forceful with my whole solidarity thing. You shouldn't be punished for having a cool boyfriend."

"But I do want to be there for Camille," I said.

"Listen," Morgan said, taking a final shuddering glance at Random Exeter. "Next Tuesday is our pre–Valentine's Day Girls' Night Out. Camille was telling me all about how the two of you used to celebrate in middle school, and she wants to reinstate it this year."

I'd forgotten how much fun those nights used to be—no boy pressure, just exchanging valentines with your friends and doing the gushy stuff guys usually only pretend to like on Valentine's Day.

"We'll go all out for Camille that night and see how she's doing. We can adjust our plans for the weekend based on her needs."

That sounded fair. The bottom line was that we both did really care about Camille—we were just showing it in slightly different (and, well, personally gratifying) ways.

As we paid for our pastries and grabbed our coats, I said, "You know, it *might* cheer Camille up to go to the dance. What if I could find her a really amazing date? Doesn't any part of you want to go too? Especially now that you've got proof positive that you're over Turtle Man in there?" I stuck my thumb in the direction of the still-making-out prep school boy.

Morgan bit her lip. "Yeah, right, who would I even go with? I'm so sick of these private school boys who think they're so great. All they want to do is trade up. It's like, just pick a nice girl and stick with her—"

"Morgan," I called, "look out!"

Her tirade was cut abruptly off when she ran smack into a tall, dark-haired guy in a red ski cap who was turning the corner from Broadway.

"Whoops!" Morgan said. "I'm sorry."

"No," the guy said, "I'm sorry." He looked at me. "Flan?"

Huh? I looked more closely under the ski cap and noticed that the tall stranger was Rob Zumberg—Terrick Zumberg's cousin, whom I'd hung out with last fall in Nevis.

"Hey Rob!" I said. "Long time no see." I looked at

Morgan, who was eyeing her collision victim pretty closely. "This is my good friend Morgan. We go to Thoney together. Morgan, this is Rob. He was our resident brilliant musician in Nevis over Thanksgiving break."

"What do you play?" Morgan asked, looking super interested.

"Guitar mostly, but I can also play the saxophone and the accordion," Rob said. He was shifting back and forth on his feet and stammering a little bit. I'd forgotten how shy he was.

"Oh my God, I've always wanted to learn to play the accordion," Morgan said. At least she was giving him some positive reinforcement!

"It's really easy to learn," Rob said. "I could show you sometime."

Then both of them looked at me, either to seek my permission to hang out with each other . . . or maybe because I was getting in the way?

"You know what?" I said, catching the vibe. "I've got to head home and read up on how to develop these pictures tomorrow—"

"Oh no," Morgan said, looking stricken. "I completely forgot to take any pictures at Balthazar." She turned to Rob and laughed. "We were supposed to do a food photo shoot and Flan came all the way down to my neighborhood to go to Balthazar and then we started talking and—wow, that was dumb."

"You live around here?" Rob asked. "I'm two blocks up. Well, if you need another food subject for your shoot, I could show you my favorite French café. It's not as over-the-top as Balthazar, but—"

"Sounds perfect!" Morgan practically exclaimed.

"Okay, I'll just—" I started to say.

"Okay, 'bye, Flan." Morgan waved, grinning. "I had so much fun!"

I laughed and waved good-bye to both of them. I could tell Morgan was having even more fun since she literally ran into Rob.

Rob Zumberg! Why hadn't I thought of him before? I mean, he was a little on the quiet side, but he was sooo into music. He was such an obvious choice for Morgan. Everything about this afternoon seemed so serendipitous. Meeting Rob right on the heels of seeing Random Exeter boy? You couldn't write that kind of stuff! As I started walking up Broadway toward my house, I had to smile. My first real match had basically fallen into my lap.

Chapter 9

WANDERING EYES

I was halfway home when my phone started ringing and the very adorable picture I'd snapped of Alex at Wollman Rink popped up on my screen.

"I've got a bone to pick with you," Alex said when I answered.

I froze in the middle of Washington Square Park South, nearly colliding with a pedicab full of tourists.

"What is it?" I asked, feeling my heart climb into my throat. "Is something wrong?" Had Alex found out about my friends wanting to ditch the dance?

"Yes," he said, sounding serious. "Something is very wrong. We've been dating for almost a month and I just realized that I have no idea whether or not you can bowl."

He was joking. My heart resumed its normal pattern as I mime-apologized to the red-faced pedicab driver.

"The thing is," Alex continued, "I'm kind of unstoppable on the lanes. So you have to be able to hold your own. I think you should probably come meet me at Bowlmor ASAP so we can resolve this."

"You only think you're unstoppable because you haven't seen my skills," I quipped back, regaining composure. "So wait, you're at Bowlmor right now?"

"Yeah." He laughed. "I'm with Saxton and Phil. And it'd be a whole lot more fun if you were here."

Hmmm, if Harper had been standing over my shoulder, she'd have told me that a boy is supposed to give you at least forty-eight hours advance notice if he'd like to take you out. But Alex had always chosen spontaneity over relationship rules. And I really did want to see him—not to mention destroy him at bowling in front of his friends.

"I'm on my way," I said, hooking a right on Eighth Street.

When I hung up the phone, I was grinning as I replayed the conversation in my head. It was cool that he was out with the guys and still wanted me to crash. And Phil was the exact friend I'd decided on fixing up with Amory! And Saxton, with his model frame and deep green eyes, might be just the thing to take Camille's mind off her Xander woes for a little while. But how to phrase this to make sure my friends wouldn't see this as a violation of their boy boycott?

NERVOUS TO MEET ALEX AND HIS FRIENDS AT BOWLMOR TONITE. COME BOWL BADLY WITH ME FOR MORAL SUPPORT?

Luckily, within minutes I had an affirmative from Amory, who wrote: I'M DOWN, BUT CAN'T PROMISE I'LL BOWL BADLY—BOWLING TEAM CAPTAIN SEVENTH GRADE!

Two minutes later, Camille said: BEATS STUDYING FOR MY ART HISTORY EXAM ANY DAY. C U SOON. . . .

Perfect! And I'd thought the Morgan/Rob connection had fallen into my lap. Something in the cosmos must have wanted me to be a matchmaker. I should probably start my own business, get a Web site—

"Flan." Amory interrupted my thoughts at the swinging door to Bowlmor. "Think I can bowl in these?" She pointed at some truly amazing hot pink patent leather Betsey Johnson platforms. "I'm not so into the eyesore of the bowling shoe."

"If you can bowl in those, you might become my fashion idol," I said, giving her a thumbs-up. "Good timing," I said. "There's Camille."

Both of us leaned in to tag-team air-kiss Camille, whose hazel eyes looked bright under her lavender velvet hat. "So I haven't cried yet today," Camille said. "That's good, right?"

"Good! Great!" Amory and I cooed as we stepped inside the jerky red elevator that would spit us out at the lanes. Having a brokenhearted friend, I realized, was kind of like raising a small child. It took a village. And every minor moving-on achievement felt like a giant leap for womankind.

Once inside Bowlmor, we were bombarded by flashing disco lights, pumping eighties music, and the strangely pleasant scent of old leather shoes. As Camille and I ordered matching size-eight red-and-blue bowling kicks, Amory impressively avoided the shoe exchange altogether.

We grabbed a round of diet cherry Cokes from the bar and scoped out the scene for Alex and his friends.

"There they are," I said, pointing to the far lane, where Alex was programming the computer with names.

"Whoa," Amory said, fanning herself. "Who's the Adonis? He's almost as amazing looking as my shoes." She nudged Camille. "Do you *see* that guy?"

Camille nodded, though she wasn't even looking at Saxton. "Mmm," she mumbled without conviction. "He's cute."

"Hey guys," I called out to Alex and his friends. "I brought company."

"Oh," Alex said, taking in the even numbers. "Cool. Uh, Camille and Amory, these are my old lacrosse buddies, Phil and Saxton. Hey, Amory, aren't you into acting? You should talk to Phil. He's a pro."

Phil laughed. "I spent eight hours today 'working' as an extra on the Bohn Brothers' new apocalyptic movie in the Meatpacking District. I'm now the resident expert on how to collapse from radiation poisoning."

"At least you got to go out dramatically," Amory said, typing her name in under Phil's on the computer screen between the lanes. "My last part in the school play was as a corpse."

As Phil motioned for Amory to grab a seat next to him and started in with, "Let me tell you about my first role as a corpse," I looked at Alex. Had my boyfriend just jump-started the exact match I'd been about to initiate myself? Speaking of perfect matches! I pulled him in for a quick kiss.

"Hey you," he said into my ear. "You look pretty sweet in those bowling shoes. Too bad they won't help you beat me."

"I'll accept your apology for underestimating me after the game." I grinned, but my smile quickly faded when I looked at Camille, who was looking at her feet and twiddling her thumbs. I felt a physical pain at seeing my most fun friend having the least amount of fun imaginable.

"So, Saxton," I said, scrambling for conversation, "what position did you play in lacrosse? Camille and I just finished a pretty intense field hockey season."

"Cool," Saxton said, fixing his gorgeous eyes on Camille. "I was left forward; what'd you play?"

"Not very well," Camille responded.

Saxton nodded politely, but then said, "I think I'm gonna go grab a heavier ball."

The game got under way without any more painful moments with Camille. I was definitely enjoying watching Alex, who was, true to his boasts, by far the best bowler in our game.

"Okay, okay," I said, sidling up behind him after three straight rounds of knocking down only one or two pins. "I was all talk. I haven't bowled since back when it was still okay to use bumpers. Got any tips, Master of the Strikes?"

"I knew it was only a matter of time before you'd come crawling back to me," Alex joked. "Okay, the thing about bowling that most people forget is that halfway through the set, the scoreboard screen tells you exactly how to position your next ball toward pins you need to take out." We walked out to the line for my second roll. Alex stood behind me. "See, if you're looking at a six-eight-nine lineup, you want to look at the ball like this."

I wasn't entirely sure what he was talking about—though I did like his hands over mine on the ball—but I sure wished there was a magic screen somewhere telling me how to position my friends toward the right guys. Despite my confusion, with Alex as my good-luck charm, I managed to take out six whole pins that time.

"Oh my God," I exclaimed. "Bowling is so much more fun when you score!"

I looked over at Camille, who was fixated on watching the balls whirr out of the machine. Sigh. At least Amory and Phil seemed like they were hitting it off. I couldn't hear their conversation, but they were both making really exaggerated facial expressions and gesturing wildly with their hands. In just a few hours, I'd found a music freak for a music freak and a thespian for a thespian. I guessed Camille's case might just take a little bit more special attention. I wondered if I knew any guys who were desperately heartbroken and looking to be fixed up. . . .

During my next round of bowling, I'm sorry to say,

I did not achieve the same success I had immediately following my lesson from Alex.

"I'm starting to think you might just have to stand up there with me every time I bowl, like a tandem coach on a skydive," I said.

Alex nodded. "I have no problem with that."

Since it was now sort of a pattern with me to have a sweet moment with Alex and follow it up with a guilty glance at Camille, I looked over at my friend again. Oh good, she was talking one-on-one with Saxton!

I stepped closer to stealthily eavesdrop, but as soon as I tuned in to their conversation, I actually wished I hadn't.

"When he broke up with me," Camille was saying, her hand over her heart, "it was like a piece of me died. I've been walking around in a daze every since. Like I'm not even awake. Do you know what I mean?"

Saxton was nodding, but I could tell it was less of a sympathetic nod and more of a how-quick-can-I-bail-on-this-convo kind of nod. He looked at the screen and sprang to his feet.

"It's my turn," he said briskly. "I'll, uh, I'll be right back."

Camille didn't really seem to notice Saxton leaving or me plopping down in his seat. I put my arm around her.

"You know what the most fun thing about bowling is?" I said.

Usually Camille would have jumped to reply, "Obviously, watching everyone's butts." But today, she missed her cue.

So I had to use my fingers to rotate her head toward Saxton. He was bending over to bowl in some very fitted Diesel jeans.

"Now," I prompted, "isn't *that* more fun to look at than the ball-return machine? Don't you think he's hot?"

Just then, Alex appeared, holding a plate of jalapeño poppers with a stiff look on his face. He sort of half held out the plate to us, then turned and offered some to Amory and Phil, first. That was weird.

Uh-oh—he hadn't heard me talking to Camille, had he? He couldn't really think I meant *I* was into Saxton.

It was time for my last frame and I nodded at Alex to join me. He didn't wrap his arms around me this time; he just told me which direction to aim for.

"Is everything okay?" I asked, while both of us faced the pins.

"Of course," he said. "Why wouldn't it be?" His voice sounded normal, but I wasn't convinced. I didn't want to make a big deal out of it; I could definitely just have been being paranoid.

After the game, when everyone grabbed their stuff and took the elevator back down to the street, he gave me a good long kiss.

"Saxton and I both live uptown," he said. I couldn't help wondering whether he was trying to gauge my reaction at the mention of his friend. "You'll be okay to get home if I share a cab with him?"

"Sure, yeah," I said. "Study date tomorrow?"

"Cool," he said. "See you then."

Camille, Amory, and Phil all shared a cab down the east side, but since I was going west, I decided to walk. I sort of wanted to clear my mind about how the night had gone. At least the Phil and Amory thing had felt like a success. And when Alex and I were bowling at the beginning together, I'd been having tons of fun. I just hoped I hadn't screwed anything up by trying to get Camille to focus on Saxton.

My cell phone buzzed and I pulled it out, hoping to see Alex's face on the screen, but it was a text from Morgan.

I'd forgotten all about her pseudo-date with Rob. I hurriedly read her message:

BE HONEST: WAS THAT WHOLE "RUN-IN" A PREMEDI-

TATED SETUP? HE'S NICE AND ALL, BUT I DON'T NEED YOUR PITY, FLAN. IT'S EMBARRASSING.

What? That was my least tactical fix-up ever! How had she gotten that idea? But knowing Morgan, this hiccup would seriously hinder any future attempts I might make at fixing her up by Valentine's Day. I guessed I was just going to have to find the *perfect* guy to make it up to her. But if not Rob, then who?

Chapter 10

TWO CUPIDS ARE BETTER THAN ONE

On Wednesday, I showed up to my study date with Alex lugging two big tote bags full of books. I had tests in three of my classes over the next week, but lately the only work I'd been doing was Cupid's.

We'd agreed to meet at Westville café in my neighborhood, a tiny hole-in-the-wall that sold local art off its walls and had a never-ending stream of West Villagers rushing through its velvet-curtained entrance. The place was famous for the number of gourmet hot dog options on the menu, which was surpassed only by the number of body piercings sported by the waiters. I liked it because of the seasonal veggie plates, massive pots of tea, and out-of-this world carrot cake.

I grabbed a table by the window and was in the midst of talking myself into skipping the meal and moving straight to dessert, when the door chimes jangled, the velvet curtain parted, and my Prince of New York stepped into the bustling restaurant.

I once overheard my mom tell my aunt that every time my dad walked into the room, even after all these years, she still felt a little bit of a rush. I'd been about ten at the time, and remembered making a theatrical gagging motion while sprinkling crushed red pepper flakes on my microwave popcorn. But now, watching Alex scan the tiny restaurant for my face—then light up when he spotted me—I totally understood where my mom had been coming from. Something about the sensation made me feel really lucky to be exactly where I was.

"That's quite a load of books," Alex said, taking off his peacoat and black Agnès B. scarf and sliding into the seat across from me.

"Maybe it only seems like a lot because you didn't bring *any*." I laughed. "Don't you ever have homework?"

Alex shrugged. "You say 'study date,' I hear 'alone time.' " He leaned over the table to kiss me. "It is sort of hard to reserve you sans entourage sometimes."

"Hey," I teased, sliding down so Alex could hang his coat on the hook next to mine. "It takes an entourage-haver to know one."

"Touché." Alex laughed.

I was eagerly awaiting an appropriate moment to pump him for details on Phil. Amory had practically bombarded me after French this morning for information about Phil's status, relationship history, mother's maiden name, blood type, etc.

The waiter arrived, tongue ring flashing, and delivered Alex's medium-rare cheeseburger, no onions, and my large, gorgeous three-tiered slice of carrot cake. In fact, it looked so amazing that I took out my well-worn camera to snap a few pictures for the food assignment in my photography class.

Alex raised an eyebrow at me. "I know you like cake, but what are you now—the dessert paparazzi?"

"It's for a class," I told him. "And don't make fun of my crappy camera. It's practically vintage. Here, take a look." I pulled out the portfolio of Balthazar shots I'd developed in the darkroom at school earlier. Spread out on the empty table next to us, all the black-and-white photographs of shiny croissants, dramatic layered napoleons, and crusty brioches did look pretty striking.

Alex examined the pictures and then me. "You took all these yesterday? And developed them today? I'm impressed."

"Thanks," I said, glad that he thought they looked okay. "Morgan and I went to Balthazar after school yesterday. I didn't know the pics were going to turn out so well. I've never worked in a darkroom before."

I realized I was blushing. Even though I was really into the class, I felt sort of funny talking about it to Alex so seriously. So instead of getting all technical, I found myself blabbing about my *other* recent hobby.

"I left the restaurant with a roll of pictures," I said lightly. "Morgan left with a date. Well, it was sort of an impromptu date. And it didn't even turn out that well. She actually got sort of mad at me because—"

I looked up and could tell that I'd lost Alex somewhere along the way. He was giving me that smile that meant he was just this side of utterly confused.

"Hey," I said, changing the subject, uh, slightly. "Have you talked to Phil since last night?"

"Phil?" Alex squirted Tabasco sauce on his burger and looked even more confused. "I figured you'd be more interested in knowing about Saxton—"

"Nah," I accidentally interrupted him. "I figure that's a lost cause."

Alex didn't respond. He seemed to be taking a really long time to chew.

"Oh my God," I said, clapping my hand to my forehead. "I meant it seemed like a lost cause *for Camille*. And I was asking about Phil because Amory was into him. You didn't think I was—did you think I was . . ." I trailed off.

"Interested in them?" Alex said, putting the remains of his burger down to wipe his hands. "I don't know."

"Alex," I said, putting my hand over his. "Not even close. You have no reason to be jealous. This whole thing started because—"

"What whole thing?" he said.

I realized then that I hadn't really voiced my master plan to anyone since SBB concocted it on the fly behind the cafeteria vending machines. I took a deep breath.

"Well . . . I'm sort of on a mission to hook all of my friends up with dates before Valentine's Day." There, I'd said it. It didn't sound *that* crazy.

"That sounds crazy," Alex said, shaking his head. "I mean, your friends are great, but come on—some of them are pretty picky when it comes to guys."

"I thought being picky was a good thing," I said coyly. "That's how you ended up with me."

"Fair enough." Alex winked at me. "But why is it your job to find everyone a date?"

There was a time when I would have been too embarrassed to admit the girly truth to my boyfriend. There was a time when I might have come up with a

really far-fetched story to explain it away. But tonight when I looked at Alex, I knew he'd appreciate total honesty the most.

"The thing is," I stammered, "after Xander and Camille broke up, my friends rallied behind her and . . . I know it sounds dumb . . . but they wanted us all to swear off guys for Valentine's Day."

"But you're not going to do that," he snorted, then paused. "Right?"

"Of course not," I said, forcing myself to look him in the eye, even though I was nervous. "I've been really looking forward to spending Valentine's Day with you. I just thought that if my other friends had guys that made them feel . . . you know . . . like you make me feel, they'd get over the whole boy boycott and then we could all just have an awesome time together at the dance."

"So that's why you brought the girls last night," he said, processing my insanity.

I nodded. "And that's the *only* reason I was asking about Phil and Saxton . . . and uh, checking out Saxton's butt."

Alex wiped his forehead with the back of his hand. "Well, *that* is a relief. I was wondering if I needed to be doing squats or something," he joked.

"So even if you don't manage to find dates for the

entire student body before next week, can we still spend Valentine's Day together?" Alex asked as I doggie-bagged the rest of my carrot cake to bring home to Noodles.

We shook on it. As he helped me into my coat, I realized that yet another study date had passed without either of us cracking a book. At least I'd come clean to Alex about the reason for my interest in his friends. And I *had* snapped that shot of the carrot cake for my photography class.

Outside, the night street was cold and quiet and we walked to the end of the block listening to our feet clack in unison on the pavement. The windows of the West Village storefronts were mostly dark, but you could still see signs of Valentine's Day in the displays.

Alex put his arm around me. "I guess the good-boyfriend thing to do would be to offer some help on the matchmaking front."

"Think of the perks!" I said happily. "If all our friends are hooked up, we'll have so much more time to hang out with each other."

"So you want me to talk to Phil about Amory?" he asked. "And I wouldn't necessarily consider Saxton and Camille a lost cause. I don't think her pout stopped him from thinking she was pretty cute."

As we turned the corner onto Perry Street, I faced Alex and put my arms around his neck. At that moment, we might have looked to anyone else like one of a million clichéd pairs caught up in pre-Valentine's bliss, but when Alex leaned in to kiss me, I felt like we were the only couple in the world.

Chapter 11

THE PLAN GOES PUBLIC

In the halls the next morning, I could tell that Morgan was keeping her distance from me. Even though I'd apologized via a really funny e-card yesterday, we were giving each other some space. I was still getting used to Morgan's somewhat fiery temper, and knew that usually her little flare-ups lasted only about as long as a coat of mascara.

But two days after our tiff over Rob, her air-kiss didn't have its usual warmth, and she still hadn't shown me how her latest batch of photos turned out.

By lunchtime, I was anxious to set things right. When all my friends were seated at our table, I marched into the cafeteria with a peace offering of chocolate-covered strawberries, a bottle of her favorite Teavana iced tea, and a plan.

Just before I sat down, Kennedy walked by, glanced at the tray of chocolate-covered strawberries in my hand, and snickered. "At that rate, someone's not going to fit into her Valentine's Dress."

"Oh, I get it," I said evenly, relishing the fact that after so many years, I was finally able to snap back at Kennedy without breaking a sweat. "I guess the concept of sharing would be foreign to me too, if I had as few friends as you do."

"Slamming comeback," Amory whispered when I sat down at the table. She popped a strawberry into her mouth. "You're getting good at the Thoney social wars."

"I've definitely had enough practice," I responded, passing around the tray. "Who wants?"

"Thanks, Flan," Harper said, helping herself. "What's all this?"

"I have a confession to make," I said, meeting Morgan's eyes. She looked like she was s-l-o-w-l-y thawing out.

"What's up?" Camille asked, looking up from the notebook she'd been doodling in. Hey, that was classic Camille—I was glad to see even the smallest shift away from the droopy-eyed, catatonic woman of the past few days.

Here went nothing. For courage, I channeled last night's memory of getting Alex on board with my matchmaking effort—and the very amazing kiss that had come afterward. I took a deep breath.

"I promise I did not premeditate that run-in between you and Rob the other night, Morgan," I began. "But the truth is, when we bumped into him and I introduced you guys, I *did* think you two could hit it off. I know you don't agree, but I need you to believe that I didn't go behind your back."

Morgan sighed. "It didn't seem like something you would do," she said. "It's just that you rushed out of there so fast, I felt abandoned, like you just pawned me off on the first guy that came along."

For the record, this was not exactly true. From the way Morgan latched onto Rob, I'd thought she'd be thrilled to air-kiss me good-bye. But since I figured this was just her hurt pride talking, I said:

"Not even, Morg. Rob's so into music, I thought—"

"Most people on earth are into music," Morgan said. "Would you pawn me off on most people on earth?"

I looked at my other friends, whose faces indicated Morgan had a point. This was not going so well. Maybe I needed to find a new way in.

"The other day at the spa," I said, fiddling with the stem of a strawberry, "you guys were all so into the boy-boycott idea. I know I'm odd girl out because I want to spend Valentine's Day with Alex, but it's more than that. I want to go to the dance with all of you." I turned to Morgan. "The Rob thing happened by chance, but if I admitted that I have been thinking about fixing you guys up with dates for Valentine's Day—would you hate me?"

The table was quiet. No one looked ready to hurl a chocolate-covered strawberry in my face, but they also weren't jumping up and down with joy.

After what seemed like an eternity, I sensed a different kind of commotion out of the corner of my eye. When I looked over at the entrance to the cafeteria, I saw a girl with black pigtails and a green beret waving her arms at the French teacher, Madame Florent. The bereted girl was shouting in French—and I caught a few very choice slang words that they definitely didn't teach you in language classes at Thoney.

Omigod, was that SBB? She'd totally dropped off my radar the past couple of days. I sort of assumed she'd gotten tired of her undercover student project and rented *High School Musical* for research. Wrong. SBB's high school stamina was still going strong, and today it seemed refocused on playing as a foreign exchange student.

I looked at my friends, who still hadn't responded to my matchmaking proposal, and weighed my responsibilities.

"I totally forgot I have to check on something in

the darkroom," I said, slinging my bag over my shoulder. "Why don't you guys think over what I said—I'll be back in a few minutes and we can discuss."

Before they could answer, I hurried toward the spectacle of my starlet pal. I loved her, but the girl was like a wildfire. She needed to be managed before she spread.

By the time I reached her, Madame Florent had exited the scene and SBB was red-faced and huffy.

"Thank *God*," she cried when she spotted me. "Where have you *been*?"

"Shhh," I whispered, looking around at my classmates, who were taking a keen interest in the loud, kneesock-wearing girl who slipped a little too easily in and out of her French accent. "Maybe we should go somewhere more private." I tugged her back into the cafeteria and we ducked behind the vending machines.

"Good, yes, I can work in this space," SBB said, closing her eyes and breathing deeply. "It comforts me. And I have never needed comfort like I have these last few days. Why didn't anyone tell me how hard high school is?"

I laughed. "I rest my case of the past six months."

"At least you're a good student," SBB moaned. "I thought this research was going to be all about navigating the social jungle, but ever since I enrolled in this awful school, they've been springing these assignments on me. I failed my French test this morning. Do I look like the type of girl who can afford to fail a simple French test?" she wailed. "Look at me."

"It's hard not to," I said, taking in SBB's wild argyle knee socks, skinny tie, tortoiseshell glasses, and the large black mole she'd drawn in over her lip. "What are you going for with that look, early-nineties Cindy Crawford?"

"Hello—*French foreign exchange student*? Which is why it is not cool that I flunked that test today. Now Madame wants to call my mother! Imagine Gloria's reaction if a high school teacher called her to talk about my grades. Uh-uh, no way!"

As SBB rattled on about her academic struggles, I sneaked a peek at my friends around the corner of the vending machine. I was getting strangely used to the view from here. They looked engrossed in a conversation, and I really wanted to be over there to make sure it was going in the right direction. One pessimistic remark from Morgan could throw off the gravity of the whole table and send them back over to the dark side of the boy boycott.

"So I gave Madame your cell number." SBB was still talking. "So you'll remember to pretend to be my mother when she calls, right?"

"Huh?" I said, tuning back in. "You want me to what?"

"Is someone back here?" A throaty voice, followed by an unwelcome face appeared behind the vending machines. Willa Rubenstein looked positively devilish in her red Stella McCartney sweater. "Flan? Did you get a part-time job stocking the vending machines?"

SBB stepped forward and before I could stop her, she adjusted her beret and piled on the Frenchy. "I vas lost." She shrugged. "I am new and Flan iz helping me find my way to ze class."

Willa looked at SBB, then at me, then back at SBB. "Honey, if you want to get to know your way around Thoney, I'd suggest a better tour guide. *Au revoir.*"

After the she-devil disappeared, SBB winked at me. "I know you hate her, but don't you love how helpful she is to my research?"

I groaned and dragged her out from the vending machine hideaway just as the bell rang to announce the end of lunch—and the end of my chance to talk to my friends about Valentine's Day.

SBB was oblivious. She was tugging on my arm and looking at me with wide eyes. "So you'll help me, right? I need to focus on fitting in—not French class."

I was flustered by Willa and bummed at the sight of my friends heading up the stairs without me, so without thinking I jerked my arm away from SBB.

"Look, I don't really have time to be your mother right now, SBB. If your French is bad enough that you fail a French test, maybe you should have picked a smarter cover." I nodded at her outfit. "Anyway, you're drawing way too much attention to yourself to fit in here. I have to go."

I knew I'd left her stranded in the hallway looking stricken, but she wasn't exactly making it easy to help her. Plus, I had my own issues to take care of, not the least of which was the chemistry test I had to take right now.

I rushed to my locker to grab my periodic table, and when I opened it up, two notes fell out.

The first one was scrawled on loose-leaf paper in Amory's signature purple pen:

> *Okay, okay, we've agreed. matchmake us. May the best date win.*
>
> *XO, Table Four*

The second note was a postcard with a photograph of an old darkroom with black-and-white prints hanging to dry. On the back, it read:

It's coming into focus how great you are. Be my valentine?

Always,

Your secret admirer

My heart skipped a beat. Alex must have been thinking about the photos I'd showed him from the Balthazar shoot. I loved that he understood perfectly how important photography was to me.

If he could make me this swoony over a simple card, I couldn't wait to see what our first Valentine's Day would be like.

Oh, shoot. I'd been too busy to think about my (lack of a) gift for Alex until this little reminder. Valentine's Day was exactly a week away, and the only thing I had to show Alex how much he meant to me was the mocket I'd bought with SBB and Camille. It was more like a gag gift. The pressure was definitely on to find something deserving of a guy who left swoonworthy love notes in lockers.

Chapter 12
LOOK WHAT BLEW IN FROM THE WINDY CITY

With the stress of my chemistry test behind me, I took out my Kate Spade planner to pencil in a shopping trip for Alex's gift 2.0 after school. But first, I had a meeting for the Valentine's Day Dance committee. It was ironic to be planning an event that I might not even get to go to, but it was also the perfect way to make up for my dismissive behavior to SBB at lunch. She didn't know it yet, but being dragged to an extracurricular meeting was exactly the kind of drama that would bolster her understanding of the life of a high school girl.

Just before last period, taking a cue from the note-droppers in my life, I raised—or dropped—a white flag into SBB's locker.

When I found her after school, she was tapping on the padlock, murmuring what sounded like some kind of chant into the slats of her locker.

"What are you," I said, coming up behind her, "the locker whisperer?"

"What are *you*?" she replied. "The friend abandoner? How the heck do people open these things?"

"What's your combination?" I asked.

SBB looked confused; then a flash of recognition came across her face. "Oh, that's what those numbers are for?" She rummaged through her massive yellow JanSport backpack, and when she caught me giggling, she dropped the bag with a thud and said defensively, "What? The guidance counselor told me this backpack is really good for the spine. It distributes the weight evenly across your shoulders. I'm carrying a lot of heavy books here, Flan; it's not like I can be fashion-forward every second of my life—"

"Calm, calm." I coached, putting my hand on her shoulder. "Which is why I'm going to show you how to use your locker. You can keep some of your books in there."

She sighed. "I'm sorry. I'm just stressed." She turned and pointed a finger at me. "And you didn't make it any better. I've never been *dissed* in the hallway before! And even though, from an acting perspective, it was kind of good for me, from a friend perspective, *I did not like it*."

"I know." I nodded. By then, I had opened up her

locker. It was dusty and empty, save for my little white envelope. "Which is why I'm going to make it up to you now."

"What's this?" SBB reached for the envelope. "My first note! I wonder who it's from!"

As she tore into the envelope, I had to wonder whether she'd be disappointed when she found out that it was only from me, but when she read my message, her face lit up. "You want *me* to join you at a dance committee meeting? I'm so excited—see, this is the kind of thing I had in mind when I signed up for this torture. Okay, you're forgiven!"

As I pulled a happily chattering SBB down the hall to the student activities lounge, I wondered whether I should warn her about how to act in front of everyone on the planning committee. I was about to open my mouth to put out a few suggestions, when I felt a tap on my shoulder.

"What's all this?" Kennedy asked, waving her hand dismissively at SBB. "The dance committee is an elected position, Flan, and what goes on there is top secret. You can't just bring anyone you want to sit in."

Leave it to Kennedy to be a stickler for the rules as long as they worked against me.

"This is a new student, uh, Simone," I stammered. "She just moved here from—"

"Chicago," SBB responded, working the Midwestern accent. "The headmistress matched me up with Flan, since she was a former new student who adjusted really quickly—"

"That's debatable," Kennedy said, rolling her eyes.

"You debate with your headmistress?" SBB asked innocently. "Anyway, the headmistress told me explicitly that the best thing I could do for myself would be to follow in the footsteps of a model student like Flan."

Oh boy, SBB was taking this a little far. Now Willa had joined the conversation, and she was definitely going to remember SBB's French persona in the cafeteria. I decided to do some damage control.

"I'm sure if you have a problem with Simone sitting in on the committee," I told Kennedy, "you can take it up with the headmistress."

That might be enough to shut them both up. Ever since Willa had been implicated in a treasury scandal last month, both she and Kennedy were on academic probation. There was no one who made them more nervous than the headmistress.

"Whatever," Kennedy said, unlocking the student lounge and taking a seat at the head of the table. She gestured toward the back of the room, where a lone desk was set off from the conference table. "She can sit in the back if she signs a confidentiality agreement."

"Yay! I'll have my agent fax a standard nondisclosure—I mean, I used to plan dances all the time at my old school in Chicago, but—" SBB squealed until I nudged her to shut up.

Willa took a seat next to Kennedy and narrowed her eyes at SBB. "Weren't you the girl behind the vending machine at lunch? Weren't you *French*?"

Whoops.

"I just act French for an hour before and after every French class, to immerse myself." SBB tilted her head seriously. I wished she would just stop talking so she wouldn't dig herself in any deeper, but I was too far away to nudge her again.

"So the Valentine's Dance," I said, changing the subject. A few other girls from our class had filed into the meeting, and I didn't think everyone needed to be privy to SBB's methodology. "It's one week from tomorrow, and we still don't have a theme, right?"

"What about Romeo and Juliet?" my friend Dara asked, brushing her long black hair behind her ears. She was the secretary on the student council, so she referenced her notes from our last meeting.

"Lame," Kennedy dismissed her. "Shakespeare's not sexy."

I glanced at SBB, whose face had that "ooh, I know about Shakespeare from a movie I once made" look on it. Before I could stop her, she'd climbed on top of her chair.

"O Romeo, Romeo, wherefore art thou, Romeo," She spouted off the lines so theatrically that her beret fell down over her eyes. "A rose by any other name would smell as sweet—"

"*What* are you doing?" Willa asked. She and Kennedy were the only ones in the room nasty enough to ask, but I could tell from the other girls' faces that they were all thinking the same thing.

"We learned Shakespeare," SBB said, "at my old school . . . in *Chicago.* Yeah, I took a test over it and everything."

I covered my face with my hands. Maybe this hadn't been such a good idea.

"What's your point?" Kennedy said, then turned to glare at me. "Flan, your shadow is being disruptive."

"Uh," I stalled, "I think her point is that Shakespeare is romantic, right, Simone?" I raised my eyebrows at SBB to try to get her to sit down and just observe.

"No," Willa said flatly. "I'm class president and I veto that idea. Dara, what else do we have?"

As Dara flipped through her notes, SBB got back up on the chair. "That's dictatorial!" she said, throwing out a word she'd loved since playing Napoleon's mistress in a smutty period piece. "At my old school, in *Chicago*, we always voted to democratically settle such important matters."

"This isn't your old school, in *Chicago*," Kennedy hissed. "At this school, in *New York City*, we socially annihilate people who annoy us."

I had to stop SBB before she made any more of a spectacle of herself. I knew from experience that SBB had to feel needed in order to stay out of trouble. I racked my brain for a task to keep her occupied.

All I had in my not-so-good-for-the-spine Muxo schoolbag was the portfolio of prints from my photography class. Without much of a plan, I pulled them out and slid them across the table to SBB.

"Uh, Simone," I said quietly, "I was wondering if you could help me figure out which one of these to blow up and turn in for my final project."

SBB/Simone looked flattered and immediately set to work. For three blissful minutes, she was focused on flipping through my prints, and the conversation about the Valentine's Dance got shakily back on track.

"Kisses on My Pillow, Love Me Do, Red Hot Valentine . . ." Dara listed off the uninspiring ideas for themes.

"Who came up with these?" Kennedy demanded. "They're all completely forgettable."

I glanced at Dara's notes. Kennedy's name was listed next to each of the bad ideas we'd come up with at the last meeting, but I could tell Dara would rather take credit for them herself than point this out to Kennedy.

"The ideas themselves aren't terrible," I chimed in. "It's just they're sort of vague. We need something concrete. We need a concept. After that, coming up with the ideas for decorations, music, and activities should be easy."

"What about . . ." SBB/Simone said. The room waited impatiently for her to articulate. I just hoped she wasn't going to get back up on the chair.

"What about this one?" she finally said, laying one of my photographs on the table. Of all my prints, this one was particularly well shot and well developed. It was an image of the perfect Balthazar linzertorte.

"You're right." I smiled at SBB. "This is exactly the print I should use for my class."

"Not only that," SBB/Simone said, laying on the hard *a* in *that* like a true Midwesterner, "it's also the perfect theme for the dance: *Picture Yourself in Love*." She turned to the other girls on the committee, but stayed—mercifully—in her seat. "What do you guys think? We could blow up giant classy prints of romantic city shots and hang them on all the walls for decoration. We could have one of those photo button-making machines and give the buttons out for favors."

As I looked around the table, everyone seemed pretty intrigued by the idea. Even Willa and Kennedy hadn't thought of anything nasty to say—and that was huge.

"Ooh." SBB grinned. "And you know that song they keep playing on the radio, 'Picture You with Me'? Who's that by again—that really hot guy?"

"Jake Riverdale!" Dara chimed in. "Love him."

"Me too." SBB/Simone grinned. "That could be the theme song!"

I held back a laugh. The undercover pimping of her boyfriend's new hit single was definitely SBB's best acting of the day.

The whole table spoke up so enthusiastically that it was clear everyone was on board. I couldn't believe that by the time the meeting adjourned, the details for the Valentine's Dance had totally come together.

"Okay," Kennedy huffed, clearly pissed that allowing SBB/Simone into the meeting hadn't been a mistake. "We'll meet again on Wednesday to finalize the details. *Everyone* better be here."

As SBB/Simone and I walked out of the conference room arm in arm, I leaned in to whisper, "That was *amazing*. Are you sure you didn't go to high school?"

"Didn't you figure me out?" SBB asked. "I was just channeling you, Flannie. You're my high school role model. You know the way you get when you're planning something and your nose gets all scrunched up and serious." She laughed. "Do you think they bought it?"

Looking back at Kennedy and Willa huddled in the doorway, I was sure that they must have. SBB/Simone had been so convincing—even though it was a little embarrassing to learn that I did that scrunching thing with my nose.

But just before we turned the corner, I overheard Willa's voice and froze.

"I've got cousins all over Illinois," she hissed to Kennedy. "I'm going to put out some feelers about this *Simone from Chicago*."

I realized I'd better warn Simone that it might be time for a costume change.

A few minutes later, SBB and I were waiting outside Thoney for her driver.

"Am I getting the hang of high school, or what?" she asked.

I was just about to tell SBB that tomorrow, she might even consider dressing like a normal New Yorker—instead of a professional student—when she pointed at the black town car slowing to a stop in front of us and clapped her hand to her forehead. "Shoot, is it a dead giveaway of my stardom that I'm being chauffeured home?"

I shook my head and laughed. "Are you kidding? At Thoney? Take a look around," I said, pointing to the line of town cars picking up the greater number of the girls who'd been at the dance committee meeting.

"Wow," she said. "High school and Hollywood

seem more and more similar every day. In that case—want a ride home?"

I looked down the street at the busy Park Avenue rush. It was nearly dusk, my favorite time of day in New York, and for a change, it wasn't bitterly cold outside. I shook my head and helped SBB into her car.

"Thanks, but I think I'm going to walk a bit. I've still got to find a Valentine's gift for Alex—" I caught myself. "I mean, to supplement the mocket."

SBB looked at me curiously. "Going above and beyond the mocket, huh? You must really like this one."

As she drove away, I started walking south on Park, trying to convince myself not to get too bogged down by the pressure of this Valentine's gift exchange. My family always said I had the magic touch when it came to gift giving. For as long as I could remember, every birthday and Christmas present I'd picked out had always received the most genuine oohs and ahhs out of anyone in my family. Part of that had to do with the fact that the rest of my relatives usually had their assistants do their shopping for them, but part of it also had to do with the fact that I put a lot of thought into my gifts. From the remote-control tracker device that I'd bought for my mom on eBay, to the chocolate fountain I'd given Feb for her twenty-first birthday, I always managed to come up with gifts that were personal and functional and unique.

Now, as the sun set in between the gray Midtown high rises, I moseyed in and out of the shops along Madison Avenue. I had made it all the way down to Midtown without finding anything, when I found myself in front of my favorite bookstore in the city, Rizzoli.

I stepped inside the impressive high-ceilinged shop, breathing in the crisp smell of new books and thinking that even if I didn't find something for Alex, I still wanted to check out their section on photography. I was sidling around a giant display of Valentine's Day books for children, when I hit a roadblock—a very tall roadblock.

"Excuse me," I said to the tall, dirty-blond-headed guy in a Weezer shirt. He was fully obstructing the only open path past the displays. I mean, who even wore Weezer shirts anymore? But I knew that Weezer shirt!

"Bennett?" I said as my ex-boyfriend spun around to face me.

"Flan?" he said. "What are you doing here?"

At first I felt guilty about admitting that I was here shopping for my current boyfriend—after all, Bennett and I had broken up because I was on the brink of a new romance with my *other* ex-boyfriend, Adam. Or did we break up before I met Adam? It was sort of hard to keep the timeline straight. The point was, I'd always felt a little bit of residual guilt/fear that I had broken Bennett's heart.

But looking at him now, he looked like his happy old Bennett self. Everything about him, from his chipped front tooth down to his worn T-shirt and frayed jeans, looked exactly the same as it had when I'd first fallen for him.

"Oh, you know, I'm just browsing." I shrugged. "What about you?"

From the way Bennett's face lit up, I thought he might tell me that he was shopping for his new girlfriend—not that that would bother me—but he just smiled and said, "I've been doing research on old film reels to try to learn more about the history of moviemaking. This place has a great section on old movie books. It's so cool, like a whole secret world."

"That's great," I said, wondering how genuine my excitement sounded.

Seeing Bennett all jazzed up about movies reminded me of all the ones he'd dragged me to watch last fall. He was the film editor of the *Stuyvesant Spectator*, and I'd always tried to support his passion for review writing, but let's just say after seven films about evil Russian clones, my enthusiasm had started to wane. For a second, the matchmaker in me came alive, and I thought that what Bennett needed was to be with someone who was just as into movies as he was—someone like Camille.

But then I remembered Morgan's harsh words in the lunchroom during the Rob Zumberg rift, and I pictured her standing over me saying, "A lot of people like movies, Flan. Are you going to pawn Camille off on just anyone who likes movies?"

No. I shook my head at the imaginary Morgan. I wasn't going to make that same mistake again.

So I looked at Bennett again and reconsidered my intentions. There was more to it than Bennett just being into movies. There was something specific about the *way* he approached his hobbies. He wasn't just interested in writing a good story or movie review; Bennett wanted to know the secret history behind everything he got involved in.

Which actually made him a way better candidate for someone like . . . Morgan! She was all about finding the secret anecdotes about her favorite bands. She spent more time poring over obscure music Web sites than she ever did on her homework. And she was forever telling us about which Beatle had written which song for which of his bandmates' wives. Totally something Bennett would do in his movie research. I also remembered the way Bennett had lightheartedly kidnapped and set free the frogs in my biology class last fall, when I'd been so stressed about animal cruelty. He was so laid-back that even when Morgan stressed about ridiculous stuff like extra-loud cappuccino makers at cafes, he'd be able to talk her down.

Bennett was grinning as he showed me one of the black-and-white books he'd found, and I caught a glimpse of his famous chipped tooth. Morgan *had* always had an unexplainable fondness for imperfect teeth. She claimed it was the Anglophile in her. It was undeniable: Bennett was the perfect match I'd been seeking for Morgan all this time.

He closed the book and looked up at me to see if I approved. "What do you think?" he asked.

"I think . . ." I said, grinning at him. "I think I'm wondering if you're seeing anyone."

Whoops, did that sound like a come-on?

"I mean, I've got this really great friend at Thoney, and I think you guys might be good together. That is, if you're single."

Bennett blushed and looked down at the ground. "Well, I mean, yeah, I am single. But . . . would that be weird?"

"I don't know," I said. "Would it?"

I couldn't tell from the tone of Bennett's voice whether he thought it would be weirder for me or for him. I didn't think it would be weird on my end, but I wasn't sure about Bennett. It wasn't really like me to think like this, but looking at his face, it crossed my mind that Bennett might not be over me.

Finally he shrugged. "It wouldn't be weird for me . . . if it wouldn't be weird for you."

"No," I said quickly. "It wouldn't be weird for me. It was my idea."

"Good," he said, thumbing through the books on the display case. "Okay, cool."

"Cool," I said, looking for something to keep my hands busy too. "So I'll text you Morgan's number and you can give her a call?"

"Sounds good." Bennett nodded. "Well, it was good to see you, Flan."

He gave me an incredibly awkward hug and hurried out of the store. I couldn't figure out which of us was responsible for that hug feeling so uncomfortable.

"I'm sorry, ma'am," a store clerk said from behind me. "We're closing. Did you want to take that *Mommy's Favorite Valentine* book?"

I looked down at the cartoon illustration on the

cover of the picture book I'd accidentally picked up while talking to Bennett. Not exactly the gift I had in mind.

"Uh, no thanks," I said, as she ushered me out the door to the dark street.

I guessed I'd have to put off my Alex shopping one more day. At least I'd gotten a little shopping done on Morgan's behalf. Now I all I had to do was convince her that this latest fix-up would be worth her while.

Chapter 14

WHAT WE CALL A POWER LUNCH

It was unseasonably warm the next day, so the girls and I decided to skip out from under the fluorescent cafeteria lights, grab some sushi from Haru, and park ourselves on the front steps of the Met during lunch.

Maybe it was the sunny weather, maybe it was just that it was Friday, or maybe it was the fact that I had very impressively arranged a slew of blind dates for my friends for tonight, but we were all having too much fun to think about going back to class.

Morgan had brought her inflatable speakers and was playing the Vampire Weekend CD I'd given her last week. Amory was making shadow puppets out of her sashimi. Harper was reading everyone's horoscopes off her BlackBerry, noting that all of our Romance Factor numbers for the day were abnormally off the charts. And Camille and I were participating in one of our favorite Met steps pastimes: selecting three guys off the street and playing Kiss, Diss, or Marry.

"Ooh, kiss," she said about a businessman crossing the street with an alligator Hermès briefcase.

"*What*? Diss—Camille, he's like forty."

"Forty and fiiine. Look at that luscious bottom lip." She pursed her own lips and made a smooching sound.

I pushed her playfully off the step and grinned. "I've missed this."

"What, me drooling over silver foxes?"

"You know what I mean," I said. "You being, well, you. I've been worried about you for a few days."

"It's still hard," she said. "Xander e-mailed the other day to see how I was doing, but I'm just not ready to talk yet. I'm trying to keep my mind off of it, you know?" I nodded. "Now remind me who this guy is that you're fixing me up with tonight?" she said.

"Camille," I said, incredulously, "it's Saxton. Alex's outrageously hot friend who you met at Bowlmor the other day? Don't you remember talking his ear off about your breakup?"

"Ugh." she shook her head. "Hazily. I guess I was still in a self-pity coma. Wait—I talked his ear off about Xander and he still agreed to go out with me?"

"He thought you were hot. Guys are able to overlook small flaws like emotional baggage to get a date with a gorgeous girl." I shrugged. "You're meeting at eight at Mary's Fish Camp. Wear that green leather skirt from Takashimaya, and just, uh . . . maybe try to focus on a new topic of conversation tonight?"

Camille nodded. "Got it. Okay, what about you, Harper? Who's our little yenta fixed you up with?"

Harper's cheeks flushed lightly. Even her embarrassment was ladylike. "A painter," she drawled.

I'd managed to get Trevor's number from Patch, who confirmed that he was in New York and single. I wasn't sure Trevor would remember me, but when I called him last night, he actually sounded really excited. He said he'd had some bad experiences with blind dates before, so I'd agreed to show up with Harper for the first half hour to moderate their introductions. It actually worked out perfectly, since Harper was a little wary of the whole blind fix-up thing as well. I knew once Trevor saw what a babe Harper was, and once she saw how cool and talented he was, they'd have no problem with me skipping out.

"I've never dated an artsy guy before," Harper was saying as she touched up her French manicure. "It feels so rebellious!"

"Just make sure you tell your parents that he also

graduated first in his class at Xavier so they'll let you out of the house," I coached. "You and I are going to meet at Grey Dog's at seven, and we'll have coffee with Trevor before I send you off on your own."

"What should I wear?" Harper asked.

I thought back to the image Trevor had captured in his painting. "Pearls," I said, glad that this request wouldn't be much of a challenge for Harper. "Pearls with something classy and black."

I turned to Amory, but before I could instruct her on the details for her date to see *The Adding Machine* with Phil, I spotted a familiar green beret dashing up the steps toward us.

Uh-oh. I'd been able to tone down SBB/Simone at the dance committee meeting yesterday, but I wasn't so sure I could maintain her cover in front of my friends. What was she doing here?

"Flan—here you are! I've been looking all over for you." SBB/Simone sank down on the steps. Today she looked like a schoolgirl from the fifties in an argyle cardigan, pleated gray skirt, and oxford shoes. Her hands were full of poster boards, Magic Markers, protractors, and a big Ziploc bag full of erasers. She looked like she'd just robbed a Staples store. And she clearly still hadn't figured out how to use her locker. In fact, she was so bogged down with school supplies, she didn't even notice the rest of my friends.

"After that committee meeting last night," she said hurriedly, "I decided that I need to join more clubs. That's the only way to round out this experience. So I signed up for the choir, the science fair, and the 4-H club. Did you even know Thoney had a 4-H club? Well, there's only one other member, but apparently that's all it takes to make a club so—"

Harper cleared her throat. SBB stopped talking and looked around, taking in my crew. For a second, I was sure her cover was blown. How were we going to explain this to my friends? I looked at Camille, who'd be the most likely of any of them to un-incognito SBB, but, amazingly, she seemed oblivious to the starlet in our midst.

Maybe it was because of how confident SBB was in her acting abilities. She just shifted her posture slightly, put on the Midwestern accent again, and stuck out her hand.

"I must have left my manners back in Chicah-go," she said. "I'm Simone, your new classmate at Thoney. You must be Flan's posse. She's told me absolutely everything about you."

I could tell my friends were a little thrown by a stranger knowing absolutely everything about them, especially when I'd never even mentioned having made a new friend. Still, they were polite enough to introduce themselves and act normal.

Which was more than I could say for SBB/Simone. After she pretended to learn everyone's names, she fixated back on me.

"So anyway, now I'm just stressing that I've signed up for *too* much. I feel put out, stretched thin, you know? I'm giving myself wrinkles and my face is insured. But then I remembered: overcommitments are my Flannie's specialty. So you can help me, right?"

"Um, actually," I said, looking around at my very confused friends, "I'm already a little overcommitted right now. I've fixed everyone up with dates tonight and I need to go over the details." I explained this last part slowly, to help jog SBB's memory that this whole matchmaking venture had been her idea—and that it was important to me, and my Valentine's Dance future, that everything go smoothly. Hint, hint. "Maybe we can meet up later?" I suggested.

"Oooh," she said, finally getting it. "I'll just wait here quietly until you're done."

Groan. Somehow I doubted that SBB was capable of waiting quietly for anything. I looked at my watch. We only had ten more minutes of lunch and I had a lot of dating ground to cover.

"Okay," I said. "Back to Amory. Your case is the easiest one, since you've already sparked with Phil."

"Oooh! Love those initial sparks," SBB cooed. I shot her a look to shut up.

"But what if Phil remembers me differently and doesn't like me this time around?" Amory used the last piece of her sushi shadow puppet to mime terror.

"Impossible," I said, shaking my head. "Just meet him outside the Provincetown Playhouse near NYU at seven-thirty, be your crazy self, and you'll be golden."

"Wear perfume," SBB chimed in again. "Actor boys love perfume."

"*Simone*!" I hissed.

"S*ah*-rry," she said sheepishly. "Shutting up now."

Luckily, after that, SBB stuck to her word, and I was able to get through the details of the final fix-up without interruptions.

"Morg, since you and Bennett are both crazy about Middle Eastern food, you're meeting him at eight-thirty at Moustache. You'll recognize him because he'll probably be wearing a Weezer T-shirt and, when he's waiting for someone, he always stands slightly slouched over, with his hands in his pockets."

"Oh, okay," Morgan said, sounding hesitant. "Remind me how you know so much about this guy?"

I'd conveniently decided to leave out the fact that Bennett was my ex. Morgan was already on the fence about being set up again, and I didn't want to do anything to tip the scales.

"Oh, you know, the usual," I said. "We had a couple classes together and a lot of the same friends at Stuy. He's great," I added. "You'll totally hit it off. But he likes really natural-looking girls, so don't wear too much makeup. And make sure to show up on time. He hates when people are late." I was trying to sound casual, but I could also sense the scrutinizing eye of SBB, who knew all about my history with Bennett.

Luckily, she came through for me and changed the subject. "So Flan, now that you've fixed up all your friends, do you get to spend some quality time with a special someone of your own tonight?"

"Actually, no," I said, almost wishing that I was the kind of person who could kick back with Alex tonight and not worry about how everyone's dates were going. But who were we kidding—this was me. And I'd put a lot of work into making sure everything went just right tonight.

I turned to my friends and shrugged. "I wanted to be around to check in on you guys. Did anyone notice how I conveniently arranged all your dates in the same neighborhood at half-hour intervals? Not that you'll need my help," I joked, then waited for my silent friends to reassure me.

"Of course not," Amory finally said, nodding as if to convince the other girls. "We'll be fine. Right, girls?"

"Right," Morgan said, looking nervous.

"We'll all bring our A-games," Camille said.

Under normal circumstances, I might have joked that hopefully Camille's dating A-game was better than her field hockey A-game, but she was biting her lip in this weird, nervous way, and avoiding my eyes by pretending to be very absorbed by the pedestrian traffic on the sidewalk below.

Why did my friends look so helpless and desperate? Gulp. I crossed my fingers that everything would go smoothly that night—and that I hadn't just made four big mistakes.

Chapter 15
THE MATCHMAKER'S TANGLED WEB

At seven o'clock on the dot that night, Harper and I walked into Grey Dog's café on Carmine Street in the West Village.

"He's late," Harper whispered, looking around frantically.

"You don't even know what he looks like," I said, scanning the restaurant myself. "How can you tell he's not here?"

"I just have a feeling," she said. "If he were here, he'd have an eye out for us."

"So he's fashionably late," I finally admitted. "He's an artist—he doesn't live according to the clock in the same way other people do. It's better this way—we'll sit down first so there won't be that awkward shuffle at the door. Relax. I'll order you a soy latte."

As Harper worriedly picked out a seat, I headed

over to the coffee bar. I'd picked Grey Dog's because it was a total artist hangout, funky yet casual (which seemed to fit Trevor's personality) and because the giant chalkboard menu hanging behind the counter touted a huge selection of vegan-friendly sandwiches and salads (perfect for the nutritionally conscious Harper). True, she stuck out a little in her pearls and black Ralph Lauren sheath dress, but I knew that wouldn't matter once lucky couple number one hit it off . . . assuming he ever showed up.

"Flan," a guy's voice said behind me. Phew—it was Trevor. Oh, and he was hugging me. "Wow, *you're* all grown up. You look great!"

"Thanks," I said, paying for the lattes. "My friend Harper got us a table over there. Come on, I'll introduce you."

"Oh," he said, looking a little disappointed. "She's here already? Did I misunderstand? I thought the two of us would have a chance to catch up and your friend would show up later."

Yikes, thank goodness Harper was out of earshot. She would've been out the door quicker than you could say *gauche.* I glanced at her sitting over in the corner. She'd just spotted me talking to Trevor and gave a tiny wave.

"See?" I gestured at her to Trevor. She was a

knockout, even when she looked as nervous as she did now. "Now, don't you want to meet her?"

For half a latte, I hung around Camille and Trevor's cramped table to help make sure the matchmaking ball got rolling. Trevor seemed polite, if a little bit reserved. Harper was charming, but kind of stiff.

"So what are you painting these days, Trevor," I asked, when their conversation lulled for a moment.

"I've been doing some animal portraits," he said. "In fact, do you still have Noodles? I always had this vision of painting the two of you together."

I don't know why that comment took me by surprise, but I found myself stammering, "You know who loves Noodles? Harper! In fact, she loves all animals. So much that she volunteers at the SPCA on weekends. Isn't that right, Harper?"

Harper nodded, but chose not to elaborate.

"Cool," Trevor said. "So, this portrait of you and Noodles—"

I looked at my watch. Crap! It was already seven-thirty. I was going to have to book it if I wanted to check in on Amory before she and Phil went inside the theater.

"Actually, I've really got to run. Harper, tell Trevor about your Great Dane. I think that's a puppy portrait waiting to happen. Have fun!"

I ducked out of the café quickly, leaving them both with sort of stunned looks on their faces. But it would probably be a lot easier for them to talk if I wasn't there directing the conversation, right?

On my jog over to the Provincetown Playhouse on Macdougal, I pulled an SBB and went just a little bit undercover. I wanted to catch a glimpse of lucky couple number two without Phil recognizing that I was spying on him. Even though Alex was down with my project, I didn't want any crazy-Flan stories getting back to him. So I slapped on the biggest pair of black D&G sunglasses I'd been able to pillage from my mother's accessories trunk, and pulled a feathered fedora over my head. Not total incognito, but if I stayed far enough away, I figured no one would recognize me.

Luckily, when I spotted Amory and Phil, they were way more at ease with each other than Harper and Trevor had been. Amory looked like she was doing her impersonation of Hillary Clinton, and Phil was cracking up. Awesome—they were totally picking up where they'd left off at the bowling alley. My work here was done!

I decided I even had time to run to the bathroom before I dashed over to Charles Street to Mary's Fish Camp to observe Camille and Saxton. But just as I was coming out of the bathroom, I saw Phil heading to the men's room. Amory must still be waiting outside. I dropped my eyes, grateful for the fedora's cover.

"Flan?" he asked. "Is that you? Are you joining us? Great hat, by the way."

Whoops, maybe my cover wasn't as good as I'd thought it was.

"I forgot you two were coming here tonight," I lied, unconvincingly. "I just stopped in because I, uh, really love the fountain sodas they sell at the concession stand. But I'm on my way to meet a friend for dinner. Enjoy the show!"

"Wait," he grabbed my arm. "Before you go, I have a confession to make."

Huh?

"That note you got the other day from a secret admirer? I know you thought it was from Alex, but ever since I met you at the premiere, I haven't been able to stop thinking about you." He looked deep into my mortified eyes. "My cousin goes to Thoney and I had her slip it in your locker."

"But—" I stammered. "You're Alex's friend. And Amory's my friend."

"And she seems perfectly nice, but if you told me I had a chance with you—"

"No way! No!" I practically shouted. What was happening? This guy was definitely trouble.

Eventually, I'd have to break the news to Amory, but I could still see her waiting outside the theater for her dream date to come back from an innocent trip from the bathroom. The only thing I could do right now was get out of there. I looked at Phil. "Let's just forget this whole conversation ever happened, okay? I have to go."

"Flan—wait!" he called, but I was already dashing for the back door.

Out on the street, I did a few of the calming breathing exercises that SBB swore by before an audition. I was still a little shaken up by the time I got to Mary's Fish Camp, but in order to focus on lucky couple number three, I tried to put the whole Phil fiasco out of my mind.

Come on, Camille, I thought as I peered through the window of the tiny fish shack for her long mop of hair. *Please be your charming self so I can feel like at least one date is going right.*

Finally, I spotted her and Saxton sitting at the bar and sharing a plate of mussels Provençal. She'd taken my advice and looked like a total bombshell in her green leather pencil skirt. Whoa—and was that Saxton's hand I saw on her knee? Normally Camille played the prude card for at least three dates. But on-the-rebound-Camille looked down at his hand and even gave him an encouraging smile.

Well, I guess it was finally a score for Flan the Matchmaker. This was by far the date I'd been most wary about, but incredibly, it looked like Cupid had finally touched down. I decided not to jinx it by sticking around any longer and turned south on Seventh Avenue for my final check-in of the night.

During the five-block walk to Bedford Street, my racing around finally caught up with me. I was exhausted, and although I'd been watching other people eat a lot of food, I hadn't had a chance to eat a thing myself. Assuming my checkup on Morgan and Bennett went off without a hitch, maybe I could give Alex a ring and see if he wanted to meet me for a late dinner at Tartine, our favorite French place on West Fourth.

Rejuvenated by my plan, I sped up to tackle my last order of business. The restaurant Moustache was the preferred Middle Eastern joint among city foodies and right up both Morgan and Bennett's alleys. As I turned west on Morton, I expected to find the two of them waiting in line for a table outside and making hesitant introductory conversation.

Then again, I wouldn't have put it past Bennett to

suggest they make a quick stop at some of his favorite (i.e., dusty and disgusting) West Village comic book shops. I shuddered, remembering the way my allergies always acted up in those dingy basement shops he loved so much. Then again, Morgan might be much less allergic to superhero comics than I'd been back in the day.

But when I reached the meeting spot for lucky couple #4, what I saw stopped me in my tracks.

My ex-boyfriend Bennett and my ex-boy-hating friend Morgan were leaning up against a lamppost—totally making out!

I froze, then quickly ducked behind a parked car. I didn't want to look at them, but for some reason, I couldn't turn away. Bennett was doing that thing where he ran his fingers through her hair and—whoa, why did I feel really nauseated? Suddenly, meeting up with Alex for dinner was the very last thing on my mind. My heart was racing and my palms were slick with sweat. What was happening to me?

I couldn't possibly be *jealous* . . . could I?

Chapter 16

JOURNEY TO A FARAWAY PALACE

After a night of maddening, stressful dreams in which I was on one never-ending date with Alex, who kept turning into Phil, then Trevor, then Saxton, then finally Bennett, I wrestled myself out of bed. At least in my nightmare, I had looked like a goddess in a long, flowing dress and tiara. But when I looked in the mirror, I recoiled at the reality. My eyes were puffy, my skin looked washed out, and my hair was a tangled mess on top of my head. I didn't even know where to begin.

After my unexpected Bennett breakdown outside Moustache, I'd fled the scene and made for my bed as quickly as humanly possible. I'd put my phone on silent, even though I'd sworn to my friends earlier that I'd be available all night for postdate recaps. Now I had four unheard voice messages, most of which I didn't think I could bear to listen to. I wasn't ready to hear whether Amory had found out about what happened with Phil, and I definitely wasn't ready to listen to Morgan gush about what an excellent kisser Bennett had been.

When I noticed the phone vibrating on my nightstand now, I quickly prayed that it wouldn't be her. Luckily, when I looked at the screen, it was SBB. Phew. She seemed like the most likely candidate to take my mind off the weirdness of last night.

"Flan, I need a favor," she said immediately when I picked up the phone.

"What's up?" I asked, trying to avoid looking in the mirror.

"I need your opinion on something," she said. "But I'm at an undisclosed location. I've arranged a helicopter to bring you to me. You'll pick it up at the Chelsea Piers lighthouse in half an hour."

Normally, I might have asked SBB for a few more particulars, like why the trip required a helicopter—when she said undisclosed location, she could mean anything from Central Park to Cairo—but today I just dotted on some Prescriptives undereye cream and started rooting through my closet for a pair of clean jeans. This was one of those days where someone else's drama was going to be a welcome distraction.

By ten thirty-five, I was shivering on the dock

outside the lighthouse by the Chelsea Piers, wondering whether I'd gotten the wrong information from SBB.

Just then, a dark-haired man in tight white pilot pants approached me.

"Flan Flood?" he asked, showing a perfect chin dimple when he smiled.

"That's me," I said, smiling back.

"I'm Rich, and I'll be escorting you to your friend." He was very tan and very Hollywood, as all of SBB's "helpers" had a tendency to be. She'd probably met him on the set of that air force drama she'd been shooting last month.

He gestured to the helicopter that had been hidden from view until a large ship pulled out from in front of it. I felt a bolt of excitement. I'd ridden in helicopters a couple of times before, but never in the front seat, and never next to such an absurdly good-looking pilot.

Rich helped me into the passenger seat and soon we were lifting off into the crisp blue Manhattan air.

"I hope you're not afraid to fly," he said over the roar of the propeller.

"I hope it never ends," I shouted back, holding my hair out of my face and away from the wind. The view of the city was breathtaking, and I soon figured out that we were heading due east. I thought about asking Rich where we were going, but there was something about the mystique of it all that made the ride so thrilling.

Soon, we were crossing over the East River, so I ruled out all Manhattan destinations. I wondered just how far away we were going. . . .

But Rich began to lower the helicopter just behind the giant Coca-Cola sign that marked the allegedly up-and-coming neighborhood of Long Island City, Queens. I'd never really been over here before, but I had seen it showcased on a home makeover special with my mom last week, right before she jetted off to the mineral springs at Ojo Caliente.

SBB was waiting on the roof of a brand-new high-rise building, and when we touched down, she started jumping up and down.

"Hooray," she shouted, throwing her arms around me. "You're here! What do you think? Wait—don't answer that, you haven't even seen what I'm talking about. Close your eyes!"

We waved good-bye to Rich, and when SBB had positioned me where she wanted me, she took her hand away from my eyes. "Voilà!"

As I took in my surroundings, my jaw dropped. We

were standing in a massive empty loft with floor-to-ceiling windows that faced the East River and the vast Manhattan skyline behind it.

"Oh. My. God." I said, taking in the high ceilings, gorgeous hardwood floor, and immaculate kitchen against the wall facing north. "What is this place, SBB?"

"Mine," she gushed. "All mine after last night. Well, mine and JR's too. Isn't it heaven? It's ten thousand square feet of pure real estate bliss."

"You own this?" I asked incredulously. "What are you going to do with it? Are you moving out here?"

"Duh." She shook her head. "I could never leave my town house. How would you survive without me as a neighbor?" It was true. SBB had moved into the town house diagonally behind my family's a few months ago and I loved having her literally a cell phone's throw away.

"No," she continued. "My vision is to turn this place into a supertrendy socialite center. I want to have a restaurant, a lounge, a catwalk for friends to showcase their new lines; of course JR will need a poker table, maybe a spa . . ."

"Wow, SBB, that sounds incredible," I said. "It'll be like the YMCA, except for the young and famous!"

"I don't know what the YMPA is, Flannie, but if

you think this is a good idea, I'll feel way better about the investment. There's just one problem."

"What could possibly be a problem?" I asked.

"The landing pad on the roof only parks two helicopters at a time, so getting here could be a logistical disaster. You're realistic, Flan. Do you think people would really be likely to take a helicopter ride out just for dinner or a game of cards?"

"I think a lot of your friends take helicopters like the rest of the city takes the train—but if you're worried about it, you know, there's a subway stop right outside."

"There is?" SBB sounded honestly stunned. "I have a confession to make. I don't actually have any idea where we are. Are we still in America?" She lowered her voice to a whisper, like insurgents might hear us or something.

I started cracking up. "SBB, this is Long Island City." She still looked entirely confused. "Queens? Ever heard of it? It's part of New York City. You can take the subway. It's super easy. I'll show you on the way home."

"That won't be necessary," SBB said, waving her hand dismissively. "But I'm so glad to know about this subway development in case of emergency. Flan, how did you get so resourceful? And so good at geography? Queens, huh? Who knew?"

"I'm going to start calling you the Princess of Queens," I joked.

"Ooh, and you can invite the Prince of New York to visit my faraway palace next time. How is Alex, by the way? And how did all your friends' blind dates go last night? Step over to where the future lounge will be and tell me all about it!"

We plopped down on the hardwood floor. While we munched on pita chips that SBB pulled out of her massive Lancel tote bag, I told her the good, the bad, and the ugly details from last night's date-a-thon.

When I got to the part about Phil's crush confession and Trevor's overactive interest in painting a portrait of me with Noodles, SBB clapped her hands and laughed.

"It's just sooo fitting that all these silly little boys would fall in love with you, Flannie. Here you were trying to help out your friends and it all backfires. If I wrote screenplays, I would—"

"SBB, this is my life. And it's serious! How am I supposed to explain this to Amory?"

"Listen, honey, one thing they don't teach you in that dreadful high school of yours is that men are fickle, fickle, fickle. Not that you're not lovely and amazing, but it won't be hard to shift these pawns' attention toward the proper queen by Valentine's Day.

Don't even worry about it—I'll be at the dance too and would love to help you keep their hands and eyes where they belong. You would think with how much time boy drama demands of you that your school would devote a class to actually *educating* you girls. This is the first assignment I've been excited about since I started high school."

"Okay," I said, feeling better. SBB did have the magic touch when it came to getting guys to do what she wanted. "But what about Morgan and Bennett? Am I a terrible person for getting jealous of my friend and my ex-boyfriend?"

"Oh, Flannie," SBB said, braiding my hair while she talked. "I'd worry about you if you *weren't* a little bit jealous. These are two people who you care about. It's like, you want them to get along, but you also don't want to lose your place with either one of them."

"You're right," I agreed. SBB might technically have been my craziest friend, but she could also be shockingly wise. "I guess I also feel so weird about the whole thing because I'm so crazy about Alex that I got confused last night by my feelings when I saw Bennett."

SBB stood up and walked over to the window. She looked deep in thought for a minute.

"You know how many other actors I have to kiss for my career, right?" I nodded. "And you know that JR has to do the same thing with a variety of scantily clad idiot young actresses, right?" I nodded again. "Well, I thought I was used to it—until last month, when he got cast opposite Ashleigh-Ann Martin for an untitled romantic comedy set on the moon."

I gasped. Ashleigh-Ann Martin was SBB's known nemesis. "Tell me there's not a make-out scene!"

SBB shuddered and nodded. "But this is our life," she said finally. "I've realized that if I want to hold on to my man—which I do; he's *so* hot—then I have to learn to combat my jealousy. And what works for me is a lot of good old-fashioned quality time."

"You mean you just hang out with JR?"

"Why do you think we bought this giant palace in the land of Queens? I got jealous just last night—so we came out here and met with the real estate agent, and one thing led to another. . . . You don't have to buy a loft with Alex," she said, as if I were actually considering it. "Just give him a call, reconnect, put this weird Bennett thing out of your mind!"

Could the solution to my weirdness be as simple as QT with Alex? It definitely beat moping around the house.

“Thanks, SBB,” I said. “I owe you one. Actually, I owe you more than one—”

“Promise to be the first patron at my palace when it opens, and I’ll consider us even,” she said.

We air-kissed to seal the deal.

Chapter 17

PRESCRIPTION: THE EPIC DATE

After journeying from Queens back into civilization again, I decided to follow SBB's advice. Me asking Alex out on a date was somewhat new territory in our relationship, but I bit the bullet and texted him Sunday morning:

HAVE A FUN IDEA FOR THIS AFTERNOON. MEET ME AT ELEVEN AT OUR SPOT IN THE PARK?

Alex wrote back almost instantly:

WEIRD—WAS JUST COMPOSING A NEARLY IDENTICAL TEXT TO YOU. I'LL BE THERE.

When we met up at the top of our favorite grassy hill near the east entrance on Sixty-eighth Street, there were only a few other souls braving the cold outdoors.

Alex greeted me with a kiss and an extralong hug to warm me up.

"So, what's your fun idea for the day?" I asked.

"Uh-uh," he said, "You first—your text beat mine to it."

Good, I'd been hoping I'd get to go first. I grabbed Alex by the hand and led him out toward Fifth Avenue. Just walking next to him made me instantly feel better about the whole Morgan/Bennett situation. Every time I glanced over at his stylish Bally's ski cap and killer smile, I knew that when it came to matches, Alex was the one for me.

When we got to Eighty-ninth Street, I stopped in front of the swirling modern exterior of the Guggenheim Museum.

"Aha," he said, holding open the door for me. "So she's beautiful *and* cultural."

"I was reading online about this really amazing photographer who's exhibiting her prints on the top floor of the museum. We've studied some of her techniques in my photography class. It's only on display this week."

The museum was crowded with buzzing New Yorkers, trying to keep warm with indoor activities. Since the date had been my idea, I stood in line to buy our tickets while Alex checked our coats. He held my hand as we wound our way up through the permanent collection toward the Guggenheim's top floor.

"I haven't been here in years," Alex said. "It was always my favorite museum as a kid because—"

"Because of the wacky winding ramp?" I said, and he nodded. "Me too! And my favorite painting in the whole city is right over—"

"Here?" Alex said. We paused in front of this tiny painting of a wave by an obscure Spanish artist from the eighteen hundreds. "I can't believe it. I've always loved this painting—how it captures the exact moment before the wave crashes."

I bobbed my head in agreement. "I think that's why I'm so fascinated by photography. I like the idea of searching for that one perfect instant to freeze in time."

Alex squeezed my hand. By then, we'd arrived at the top floor where the photographer, Anise Mapplethorpe, had her sleek sepia prints on display. I couldn't help taking mental notes about some prints that might be the exact style we were looking to use for our decorations at the dance. There were lots of shots of food and even more dramatic cityscape images. I was enjoying the exhibit so much that I almost forgot to see what Alex thought, but when I looked over at him, his eyes were wide.

"I can see why you wanted to come here," he said when we came to the end of the exhibit. "Now, since

I'm going to drag you back out into the cold for my portion of the date, I figure I should sweeten the deal with hot chocolate."

Carrying our two giant Guggenheim café hot chocolates with extra whipped cream, Alex and I braved the cold again as he led me back into Central Park. We stopped in front of the duck pond at one of those telescope machines you pay a quarter to look into. I looked up at Alex, trying to guess what he had in mind.

"There's something I've wanted to show you ever since we started dating. Most people I know would laugh, but this is secretly my favorite place in the city." He slipped a quarter into the viewfinder, wheeled it to a stop, and gestured for me to look through it.

I pressed my nose against the frozen metal ledge and peered through. It was fixed on the top of a high-rise apartment building, and when I adjusted the focus, I could make out a mass of twigs near the edge of the roof.

"It's a nest," I said. "It's huge."

"It belongs to the only known red-tailed hawk in Manhattan," Alex said. "Usually they like warmer climates, but this one's been living there for years."

I looked up at him. A smile spread across my face. "You're an undercover bird-watcher."

"Guilty," he said. "It's pretty hard to be a bird

fanatic in the city, especially without binoculars." He shrugged and looked through the viewfinder. "But I'll take what I can get."

"It's amazing," I said. "I wish I had my camera to take a picture."

"It'll be here tomorrow," Alex said. "What *won't* be here tomorrow is the reservation that a friend of a friend got us for dinner at Nobu tonight."

"Seriously?" I asked. Nobu Fifty-Seven was this ridiculously amazing sushi place in Midtown. I'd been there once and the tuna belly sashimi literally melted in your mouth. I loved that place, but it usually took months to get a reservation.

"Seriously," he said. "I guess the look on your face means you like the idea."

As we started to walk toward the restaurant, I couldn't believe the sun was already setting. Throughout this entire epic date, I felt like Alex and I had gotten to know each other better and better. It was cool to discover new things we had in common even while showing off our separate interests.

At the edge of the park, we paused in front of a hot dog stand to take in the view of the horse-drawn carriages outside the old Plaza Hotel at dusk.

"This is my favorite hot dog stand in the city," Alex and I both said at exactly the same time.

"What??" we both laughed. "Jinx!"

"I can't believe you just said that," Alex said, shaking his head.

"I can't believe *you* just said that. I think it's the relish—there's just something about it."

"Exactly," Alex said, and we both started laughing. "Of all the hot dog stands in the city," he said. "This feels too remarkable to me to go uncelebrated."

"What do you mean?" I asked.

"I mean, who needs Nobu when we have this coincidental love for the same random hot dog stand. I vote we ditch that stuffy reservation and take two of these hot dogs, extra relish, on a carriage ride around the park."

I didn't know any Manhattanite who would skip out on a reservation at Nobu on a whim, but then again, I didn't know anyone else in the world like Alex.

"Sounds perfect," I said. And it was.

I was in such a haze of hot dogs and happiness that I didn't even think to check my phone until I got home at ten o'clock that night.

To my surprise, I had seven missed calls from SBB and fourteen text messages.

11:30 a.m.: NEED YOU.

11:43 a.m.: STILL NEED YOU.

12:12 p.m.: DID YOU FALL INTO A SAMPLE SALE RABBIT HOLE OF SOME SORT AND NOT TELL ME ABOUT IT?

And so on.

Whoops—I felt bad that I had missed her, but I knew it was already too late to call her back. SBB required a lot of extra beauty sleep and was always in bed by the time *Desperate Housewives* ended on Sundays. Well, at least it had been her idea for me to put the Bennett weirdness out of my mind by spending the whole day with Alex. She'd understand if we just caught up tomorrow, right?

Chapter 18

CLUB FOF LOSES A FOUNDING MEMBER

Fully rejuvenated by my fantastic date with Alex, I arrived at school Monday morning feeling more committed than ever to solidifying my crew's Valentine's Dance matches.

Standing outside of Thoney, I braced the winds to make a quick call to Feb, who'd emerged from couplesville to text me a few pictures of her dancing at some purple-lit nightclub in Shanghai.

"I can't hear anything," she shouted when she picked up. "Hold on, I'm going outside."

"I'm fine, thanks for asking," I said back, holding the phone out at arm's length to preserve my eardrums from the techno music drowning out my sister's voice.

Then there was a slight drop in decibel as Feb found a space outside to say, "Good timing. It's way too hot in there to dance to another eleven-minute techno song. Chinese ravers have insane energy. Insane. What's up?"

"Can you hear me well enough now to give some boy advice?" I shouted, becoming aware of what I might sound like to the other Thoney girls filing past me into school. But I needed a second opinion on the Phil fiasco, and I knew Feb had gotten her share of love notes from the wrong guy before. She'd know better than anyone how concerned I needed to be.

"This reeks of further drama," she said, when I'd finished. "For Amory's sake, I'd cut your losses and move on. She seems cool and there are way too many other, worthier fish in the sea. Look, Kelly's got some cute friends in the city. Why don't I text you some headshots and you can take your pick for a replacement, okay? But I gotta dash—I *love* this song!"

With that, the phone cut out. As Feb headed back into her nightclub, I sighed and headed back into the doldrums of high school. It was times like this when I felt far away from my sister's life, but I knew she'd always come through with some words of wisdom and/or headshots.

"Omigod, Flan," my friend Veronica said when I passed her in the foyer. "Hot trench."

"Thanks." I beamed, realizing with a grin that, even continents away, Feb was a lifesaver in more ways than one. Sometimes, when I missed her most, I did a little retail therapy in her raid-worthy closet full of unworn clothes. Like this morning's choice of the goat-suede Dior trench I'd dug up, rationalizing that since she and Kelly had sworn off animal products, *somebody* ought to wear it.

I opened my locker to hang up my coat and found a CD and, taped to it, a note scrawled in Morgan's hand.

> *A LOVEly mix to get us in the mood for Girl Valentine's Night tomorrow. Enjoy the tunes and don't forget—no dishing about Friday's dates until we're all together!*

Sweet. Morgan always made the best mixes—and more importantly, I'd forgotten the girls and I had made that promise. This bought me a little more time to work on Phil 2.0—and to get used to the idea of hearing Morgan talk about Bennett. Things were looking up!

At my locker, I heard Dara's voice call out, "Supercute look, lady!"

I turned around to accept my second compliment of the morning, but before I could speak too soon, I realized Dara wasn't talking about my Dior trench at all. She was looking at another girl walking down the hall in a charcoal Balenciaga rubber dress that SBB and I had eyed on the runway at last month's fashion week.

Were my eyes playing tricks on me—or *was* that SBB underneath the black wig?

"Hey!" I whispered, when I was close enough to get SBB's attention. "I can't believe you got the dress. It looks *amazing* on you!"

SBB's eyes flicked over my trench coat, then looked past me down the hall. She said nothing, just kept walking toward her locker.

I followed her and put my hand on her shoulder. She shrugged it off.

"SBB," I said, feeling my nose wrinkle up in confusion.

"Don't call me that," she huffed.

"Sorry," I corrected myself. "Simone—"

"Actually, it's *Sally* now," she said coldly. "Things have changed."

"Huh? Look, I'm sorry about yesterday. I saw your messages, but it was too late to call you back. The good news is that Alex and I—"

"Zip it, Flan." She slammed her locker shut. "Do you have any idea what happened to me yesterday? I'll tell you. I ran into your favorite enemy, Willa, on the street—and she seized me. I was literally captive in her French-manicured claws. Thank God I had my wig tucked inside my Birkin for just such emergencies. Anyway, I could have sworn she was about to out me on that little Chicago fib. But instead, because she *hates* you so much, she spent all day giving me a makeover—so I could be 'cool' like her and not an 'FOF loser.' Sorry," SBB said, not sounding very apologetic. "Willa's words, not mine."

"An FOF loser?" I said. I was reeling from all this talk of Willa's seething hatred for me, but something about SBB's behavior was throwing me even more. "What does that even mean?"

"*Friend of Flan*," she said, looking around like she was making sure no one could see her talking to me in her new cool state. "After Willa put out tracers to all her bitchy cousins in Chicago, I had to scramble to come up with a story that I was just a normal girl from Hoboken. Like how I lied because you told me to, so I could seem more intriguing. I tried to call you all day, but you blew me off—and *not* for the first time since I've been at this school!"

"SBB, look, I'm sorry." I didn't like the idea of my friend spending all day with Willa, but I was trying to stay rational. Maybe instead of getting jealous again, what I needed was to schedule some QT with SBB, the way I'd done with Alex. "Let me make it up to you. Let's have lunch, just the two of us, okay?"

She shook her head. "It's just too little, too late. The thing is, after I started to go along with Willa's makeover yesterday, it was . . . fun. There, I said it. I had fun, with your enemy."

I sucked in my breath. That was harsh.

"I can't have lunch with you today." She paused dramatically. "Because I'm having lunch with Willa *and* Kennedy. They want to *include* me in their life—not keep me on the fringes of it. You never let me hang out with your friends."

"That's not true," I said, racking my brain. "You had lunch with us on the steps on Friday."

SBB rolled her eyes. "If you call wearing a virtual muzzle 'having lunch.' And that was only because I tracked you down. Because of you, I haven't had the high school experience I wanted at all. Do you know that six out of ten people at this school prefer a guy who shaves his chest? See, I'm learning things from Willa that will really help my career. When were you planning to teach me anything about being in high school?"

I didn't see what that statistic had to do with anything. And I definitely didn't see Willa as being all that in touch with the pulse of the student body here. But I could also see where SBB was coming from. Maybe I had been a bit preoccupied with my own pursuits during the past week.

"I'll fix this, SBB," I said. "Just promise me you won't let Willa suck you any further over to the underworld before I can make it up to you, okay?"

"Unlike some people," SBB said pointedly, "I don't feel comfortable making promises I can't keep."

"Sally, is that you?" I heard Willa's voice call out. "Awesome, I'm so glad you're wearing the dress. You're such a fast learner."

Shocker, Willa was being totally condescending, but for some reason, SBB seemed to be eating it up.

Then Willa glanced at me.

"I thought we agreed," she said slowly to SBB. "No more FOF-ing. It's not good for your rep."

"Sorry, Willa," SBB/Sally said. She'd lost all traces of her Chicago accent and was now another typical bitchy UES girl. "I was just saying good-bye." SBB turned to me. "So—good-bye."

Before I knew it, my best friend and my worst enemy were walking down the hall, arm in arm.

Chapter 19

IF THE VALENTINE FITS . . .

One day later, and one FOF down, the day that I'd been waiting for since I heard the words *boy boycott* had arrived. No, it wasn't Valentine's Day, but it was an important preliminary step: GVNO (aka Girls Valentine's Night Out; aka the night we'd agreed to gauge whether Camille was emotionally healthy enough to be dragged to the Valentine's Dance).

We were meeting at eight at Stanton Social, and I was the first to arrive. From the coveted back booth overlooking the entire scene, I reviewed the valentines I'd made for my friends. The sophisticated doily-laden Victorian valentine for Harper, the programmable singing card for Morgan, the sleek, modern postcard Valentine I'd picked out at Crane's for Amory, and the platonic Mad Libs love letter I'd written for Camille. When I'd bought the supplies over the weekend, I'd bought enough to make a paper doll Valentine for

SBB, but after yesterday, I'd reached the breaking point. I was so over fighting with Willa over something that should have been rightfully mine. And more than that, I was sick of trying to keep up with who SBB was supposed to be on what day of the week.

Now, as I looked around the room at the other glammed-up patrons in the restaurant—girls in flashy stilettos and Siwy jeans, and guys all freshly shaven and showing a very calculated amount of chest hair—I understood that SBB wasn't the only one in costume. To a certain extent we all were. But costume or not, I reminded myself, there was no excuse for the way she'd ditched me yesterday for Team Willa.

"Hey, there you are," Amory said as she slid into the booth next to me wearing a hot white Chloé slip dress with a plunging neckline. "Harper and Morgan are checking their coats. Where's Camille?"

"Right behind you," Camille chirped. "And I brought a guest Valentine."

She stepped aside to expose a very expertly done-up incognito SBB/Simone/Sally in a brilliant, shorter black wig and a Smart Fitzgerald patterned slip dress. She looked incredible again, but I had to muster some major willpower in order to suppress my groan. It was bad enough that she'd synced up with Willa; now she was moving in on Camille?

"Oh, hi—Simone, right?" Amory said, gesturing for SBB to sit down.

SBB shot me a nervous look. "Actually, it's Sally now. It's my middle name—Simone Sally . . . Struthers—and I think Sally's fresher, more New York, you know?"

As SBB babbled on about the very scientific explanation behind her name change, Camille pulled me aside. "I was leaving Thoney today and I spotted the poor, defenseless thing arm in arm with *Willa*. I figured since the headmistress assigned you to take Sally under your wing, I should help save her from the axis of evil. She's actually super nice—we should hang with her more often."

"Totally," I agreed halfheartedly. I searched Camille's face to see whether she was bluffing. It would be just like her to figure out who SBB was, then cover for me with a few covert winks. But Camille looked genuinely concerned about Sally's social acceptance into our clique. Exactly how preoccupied was she by all of this Xander stuff?

When we were all seated and had ordered enough Kobe miniburgers and halibut tacos to feed a modeling agency, we all passed out the valentines we'd made for one another. As I thumbed through the cards my friends had made for me, I realized that I wasn't the only one who'd personalized the cards based on distinguishing traits: all four of the valentines I received were matchmaking-related. Camille had even sketched out a scene from the *Fiddler on the Roof* as a joke.

"Okay, okay." I laughed. "I get it—you're sick of my obsession with fixing you all up with dates."

"Not even." Harper laughed. "We're just messing with you, Flan. I had a really good time with Trevor on Friday night. After you left, I even let him sketch my shoulder. He said I had remarkable clavicles."

"Oooooh," Amory teased. "You showed a boy your *shoulder* on the first date? Aren't you the girl who recently told me that boys don't buy the cow if they can get the milk for free?"

"He didn't get it for *free*," Harper said shyly. "He agreed to be my date to the Valentine's Dance." She quickly shot a look around the table. "I mean, *if* we decide to go."

"Maybe we should go," Amory said, sipping on her mango iced tea. "I'm sort of into Phil. He was so funny after the play; he was doing all these great impersonations of the characters."

Oh, crap—I *still* needed to figure out how to play off the whole Phil situation. Feb had sent a slew of pics of muscle-y Aussie men, any of whom would be a great substitution. My only problem now would be swapping Phil out without seeming suspicious. In my head, I started scrambling for a tactful way to talk to Amory, but I snapped back to reality when Morgan cleared her throat to speak.

"I know I was the loudest voice for the boy boycott last week." She looked at me and smiled. "But Flan did such a killer job setting us all up last week, I think I'm changing my tune."

"Morgan loves Bennett, Morgan loooves Bennett," Amory sang.

"We've been texting all week," she gushed.

While everyone else started oohing and ahhing over Morgan and her new love interest, I started to get that sinking feeling in my stomach again. Even in the guise of her new persona, SBB was watching me to see how I was coping.

She'd been remarkably quiet all through appetizers, but when she caught my eye, she spoke up. "So what's the problem here, girls? Sounds like you all want to go to this dance. Why the self-imposed boycott?" She flicked her eyes at me, and I felt like this was an attempt to get back on my good side.

The rest of the table had their eyes on Camille.

"What?" She finally shrugged. "It wasn't my idea to start hating all men in the first place. If you guys want to go to the dance, I'll go. I don't think Saxton's my next great love, but he'll do for picture taking."

I could tell that Camille, who thrived on being a good sport, was trying hard to take one for the team. But the fact that she didn't seem to care whether we all went to the dance or not reflected her general ambivalence toward everything these days. I wished there was a way to snap my fingers and take away the residual Xander pain.

"What about you, Sally?" Harper said to SBB, passing around a plate of fruit skewers. "Are you planning on going to the dance? Is there a special someone in your life?"

"You know, it's hard for me to date high school boys," Sally said, "because I have something of an obsession from afar with a certain movie star–pop singer. Confession: ever since I rented his film, *Demolition Dudes*, on DVD, I've been hopelessly in love with . . . Jake Riverdale."

The way she said it was so hilarious—especially because my friends all believed her pathetic crush-from-afar act—that even in my annoyed state, I had to join in with the rest of the table and crack up.

When the laughter died down, SBB/Sally turned to me and said, "You're quiet, Flan. Do you have a date to the Valentine's Dance?"

"Oh, Flan has the best date of anyone," Morgan said, shocking me with her enthusiasm. "She has this totally amazing boyfriend named Alex—"

"The Prince of New York," Harper chimed in.

"And he's crazy about her," Amory said.

It was hard to believe how much the tables had turned. Last week, my friends had been giving me death stares anytime I brought up Alex's name. Now they were cheering me on. It was funny how much easier it was to gush over your crush when your friends wanted to hear it.

"Things with Alex are great," I said, taking a final bite of my sinfully dark chocolate ice cream. "But we can hang out anytime. I'm just glad to hear you guys all get on board for the Valentine's Dance."

By the end of dinner, we'd sampled just about everything on the menu, dished on just about every boy in Manhattan, and come to the group decision that it was Valentine's Day Dance or bust. I buttoned up my Dior trench and we stepped back out into the cold.

"Which way are you headed, Sally?" Camille asked, hailing a cab.

SBB, who lived twenty feet away from me, would have offered to split a cab, but Sally squinted at me and skirted the question. She pointed at a black town car across the street. "Toward my driver. See you later!"

Everyone else grinned and called good night, but I couldn't help wondering about the icy distance between me and SBB. What if the new *Sally* didn't keep *SBB's* Valentine's Dance promise to help me keep everyone's dates fixed on the right girl? With my track record so far, I wasn't sure I could do it alone.

Chapter 20

BIPPITY BOPPITY BALL GOWNS

On Wednesday, just before last period, I was thrilled to see my phone light up with the signature ring I'd set for my favorite French fashion designer friend, Jade Moodswing. Jade was an old friend of Feb's, and when she'd been in the states for Fashion Week last month, I'd lucked into a spot as a model in her show at the Armory. But ever since Feb had become Feb'n'Kelly, our household had been lacking its token ninety-seven-pound, chain-smoking, perpetually pouting designer.

"Coo-coo, *chérie*," her hoarse voice came across the phone. "Zere is small favor I need to ask. I must jet back to Paree *ce soir*, but my suitcase iz too full to fit in—how do you say—overhead compartment. Can you pleaze take a ball gown or two off my hands?"

"Let's see. . . . Um, where do I sign?" I responded, laughing.

I ducked out of school as soon as the bell rang and hailed a cab downtown to Jade's atelier in Chelsea. I was about to press the buzzer to her studio when I spotted a familiar profile peering through the windows of a store across Tenth Avenue.

What was *Xander* doing window-shopping at the 202 Boutique in Chelsea?

Before I knew was I was doing, I'd sprinted across the avenue to spy on him from a lesser distance. Why was he lingering in front of that one mannequin? And why did he have such a forlorn look on his face?

Then it hit me: 202 was Camille's favorite clothing store in the city.

"Xander?" I asked, tapping his shoulder.

He spun around. "What?" he said. His voice sounded strained and a little defensive. "I was just—I wasn't—"

"What are you doing down here?" I wasn't trying to give him the third degree, but I realized I sounded a little bit suspicious.

"I was . . . uh . . . looking for a present . . . for my mom for Valentine's Day. But this place doesn't have much." He turned back around and glanced at an amber and garnet necklace in the window that pretty much screamed Camille. "I'll probably just go to Louis Vuitton. She likes key chains and stuff." He was rambling, clearly nervous.

"Okay," I said, trying to put him at ease. "So, how've you been?"

"I've been good. I've been fine." He shot me a look. "Why? Did Camille ask about me? Never mind. Look, I should get going. Great to see you!"

Before I even had time to wave good-bye, Xander had taken off down the street faster than a Kenyan marathon runner. I knew I needed to tell Camille about the run-in, but since I couldn't exactly make sense of it myself, I wasn't sure how to position it to her.

Slightly shaken up, I crossed back over to Jade Moodswing's side of the street. When I got upstairs, she was perched on the windowsill smoking a cigarette and talking into a headset. A team of at least ten assistants ran around the room packing up dresses, tearing mock-up sketches off the walls, and stuffing fabric scraps into a giant platinum trunk.

When Jade saw me in the doorway, she waved me over to her, then gestured dismissively at the scene. "Iz always depressing to disappear from a place like zis. Two more hours in New York, then poof, we'll be gone."

"But you'll come back soon, right?" I asked. "Fall Fashion Week's only a few months away. . . ."

"We'll see," Jade said cryptically. "In the meantime, you must promise to wear the dresses well, *chérie*. I've arranged for a few of ze girls to model the line for you so you can select ze ones you want. Come, sit by me on ze ledge and take a look. Can someone bring Flan a Pellegrino?"

"Seriously?" I asked, plopping down on the sill next to Jade. This was almost more exciting than being one of Jade's models in the Armory show. It was definitely more relaxing.

"Do you want us to cue the music?" Jade's head assistant asked from the back of the room.

"Yes, yes, we spare no expense for Chérie," Jade said.

The lights dimmed, two flutes of Pellegrino arrived, and I tried not to laugh in disbelief. When I'd woken up this morning stressing over my Latin test and silly high school boys, a private fashion show of Jade Moodswing's latest formal-wear line had been the furthest thing from my mind. Oh, life . . .

Soon enough, the models filed out of a back room, pranced down an imaginary catwalk, and stopped right in front of Jade and me to pose.

"Oh my gosh," I said, breathing in the scent of all the haute couture. "Jade, you've outdone yourself."

"You like? They are all from ze newest line. I call eet *Jewel*."

I could see why. All the dresses were jewel-tone shades—deep sapphire, rose quartz, emerald, even an iridescent opal color, which I fell instantly in love with. Each gown also had a different signature touch—from a keyhole neckline, to a darted velvet bodice, to a layered petticoat that grazed the hard-wood floor.

"These are amazing!" I said, a little breathless. "Each one is so unique, but they're still so totally you."

"I think zey are totally *you*, *chérie*. Maybe you will wear one on Valentine's Day for your *amour*."

"Actually," I said, eyeing the opal-colored gown, "we do have a Valentine's dance at school on Friday night." But then, I also couldn't stop staring at the emerald dress—or the sapphire dress. "Any of these would be perfect. I'm just not sure how to pick which one."

"Why do you have to pick?" Jade asked as the models continued to swirl around us. "To tell you ze truth, I don't really have room for any of zese. Take zem all, decide which one to wear later—give zem out to your friends as petite Jade mementos, *non*?"

My friends were all just as obsessed with Jade's couture as I was. The thought of showing up at the dance with an entourage clad in Moodswing couture made me bust out into a giant grin.

"That way," I said, rationalizing her gift, "even when you leave New York, you'll still be leaving a legacy of fantastic dress."

"*Parfait*," Jade said, snapping her fingers for an assistant to wrap up the dresses. "Everybody wins."

Blowing out a ring of smoke, Jade Moodswing might not have looked much like a fairy godmother, but I definitely felt like Cinderella. Only this time, real life trumped fairy tale, because I don't think Cinderella ever got to take four extra dresses for her friends to wear to the ball.

When the dresses were wrapped up and I had enough taffeta and silk to clothe a lesser borough, I leaned in to give Jade a thank-you kiss on each cheek. I skipped down the stairs to catch a cab. Maybe I could soften the blow of the cryptic Xander story by offering Camille first choice of the dresses for the dance.

Oh, shoot! The dance! With all the private fashion show excitement, I'd completely forgotten that I was supposed to go to a committee meeting today after school. And when I checked my cell phone in the taxi, I had the threatening text message from Willa to prove it.

IF YOU DON'T START PULLING YOUR WEIGHT, FLOOD, I DO HAVE THE AUTHORITY TO REMOVE YOU FROM THE COMMITTEE. PUBLICLY DETHRONED AT THE VALENTINE'S DANCE—WOULDN'T THAT BE EMBARRASSING?

Chapter 21

SOMETIMES IT TAKES THREE TO TANGO

On Thursday morning, I woke up before my alarm clock to the sound of our repeatedly ringing doorbell.

"Could somebody get that?" I shouted in the general direction of the rest of my family. "Oh, right," I remembered aloud. "I'm the only one who's ever actually home. No offense, Noodles."

Yawning, I pulled on a sweatshirt and thumped down the stairs, thinking that whoever was cruel enough to ring someone's doorbell so many times before 8 a.m. had better have a pretty good excuse.

For a second, I thought that it might have been my dad. Even with his insane travel schedule, he tried really hard not to miss a Valentine's Day. But I knew that he had an important business meeting/golf tournament in Maui all week, for which he had already apologized profusely.

When I opened the door, I was greeted by a stranger in a Yankees cap.

"Can I help you?" I asked.

"I doubt it," he said flatly. "But they're paying me to help you." He reached behind him to pick something up off the stoop. Unceremoniously, he handed me the most enormous bouquet of red roses that I had ever seen.

"Omigod," I gasped.

"Omigod is right," the deliveryman said. "You must be pretty special. This guy got you the deluxe. Sign here." He held out a clipboard.

"I can see that," I said, signing my name and nearly buckling under the weight of the vase. "Happy Valentine's Day!" I said, overflowing with romantic wishes for everyone around me.

"Yeah, yeah," the guy said, starting down the steps. I guessed if I had his job, I might not have been so cheery, but as it was, I couldn't wait to read Alex's card—or to set the massive vase down before I dropped it.

The card was simple and white, but the message inside was anything but:

I know you think that I'm a guy who always
breaks a rule.

But to deny you red roses on Valentine's day, I'd
have to be a fool.
Please don't expect a lot more verse from your
nonpoet boyfriend,
Just wanted to give you a romantic day from its
beginning to its end.

Can't wait to see you tonight.
—A

For the first time in my life, I was almost glad that my family wasn't around. If they'd seen me blush this hard over a love note from a boy, they never would have let me live it down.

By the time I met up with Alex after school, I'd stopped blushing and was just really excited to hang out with him. It had been such a long, fun, busy week of friends and fix-ups and dance coordinating, but now I was ready to dedicate my entire night to my valentine.

He'd left me a message to be dressed and ready to hit the town at seven o'clock, but at a quarter to seven, I was just getting around to wrapping the gift I'd rush-ordered online earlier this week. Five minutes later, I zipped up my brand-new soft pink flapper-style cocktail dress, and at six fifty-nine, I was smacking on my signature Chanel lip gloss. I had never been so punctual, but Alex always was, so I wasn't surprised when the doorbell rang just as I was blotting my lips with a tissue.

I dashed down the stairs and flung open the door. Alex had never looked better. He was wearing a dark gray Calvin Klein suit, a light pink button-down, and these really unique Euro-style black loafers.

"Whoa," we both said at the same time, taking in each other's outfits.

"I love your shoes," I said.

"You look beautiful," he said, stepping inside and looking around. "Do you still have the house to yourself?"

"Um, yeah," I said, wondering what he had in mind.

"Good." Alex turned around and picked up two hefty paper bags from Zabar's. "Point me toward your kitchen. I'm making us a Valentine's feast."

"Be gentle." I laughed, thinking about all the take-out food our house had seen in the past few months. "This room doesn't get a whole lot of use."

But as I led him back into our kitchen, I was secretly thrilled that he'd put more energy into planning our date than just making a reservation at some fancy restaurant. Things were already off to a really romantic start.

As it turned out, Alex was a real pro in the kitchen, which I added to the list of things that made him incredibly attractive. While he unloaded the groceries, I got to work picking out the music. Luckily, I had Morgan's latest mix on my computer, so I didn't have to play my typical embarrassing lineup of *American Idol* tunes.

"Do you like Al Green?" I called from the stereo in the living room.

"Are you kidding? Al Green invented the love song. He *is* soul."

"I'll take that as a yes." I laughed, pumping up the volume on the speakers. "Can I help you make dinner?" I asked, even though I hardly recognized most of the food Alex was unloading on my counter.

"Definitely," he said. "Do you know how to make aioli?"

"A-what-i?"

Alex kissed me and handed me a head of garlic and an apron. "Here," he said, laying down a cutting board. "I'll show you."

He wasn't kidding. For the next forty-five minutes, Alex showed me how to turn olive oil, an egg, and some garlic into the most amazing dip I had ever tasted. While I sliced the City Bakery baguette and some farmers' market veggies for the dip, Alex pan-fried an entire fish, filling the kitchen up with incredible smells of rosemary and sage.

By eight-fifteen, we were sitting down to a huge spread of amazing-looking food. It was the most romantic and intimate meal of my life—everything was so perfect that it almost made me nervous.

"Is something wrong?" Alex asked. "Did I overcook the fish?"

"Not at all," I said, taking a bite of trout as proof. "Everything is perfect."

"Just wait," he said. "There's more."

"You always say that." I laughed.

"And don't I always come through?"

By the time we finished eating, I was ready to give Alex my gift. But right when I stood up to excuse myself and run upstairs, the doorbell rang.

"I'll get it," Alex said. Before I could protest, he was opening up the front door to let in a small man wearing black yoga pants and a black button-down shirt.

"Flan," Alex said, registering the very confused look on my face. "This is Paco. He's the best salsa teacher at Broadway Dance."

"No way," I gasped, guessing at what he was about to say.

Alex nodded. "I know you're always talking about how fun it'd be learn salsa, so I thought this might be a good time for a private lesson."

Paco stuck out his hand and looked at me seriously. "Nice to meet you, Ms. Flood. I hope you're ready to sweat."

Paco wasn't kidding. For the next hour and a half, he made us work up a pretty continual glow. Alex had some natural moves, but I was, embarrassingly, a little bit of a klutz. I kept tripping over my own feet and making Alex stumble with me. Alex thought it was pretty funny—Paco, not so much.

"Eyes up," he kept yelling at me. "What's with the elephant feet! Are you even listening to the music?"

Some girls might have gotten frustrated, but the tough love was good for me. By ten o'clock, I could make it through one whole dance routine without making either Alex or myself fall down.

At the end of our lesson, Paco turned to Alex. "She worried me at first—but she really stuck with it. I like it."

Alex laughed. "Well, thank you. I like it too."

After we showed Paco to the door, I turned to Alex.

"Thank you so much," I said. "I knew I was going to have fun no matter what we did, but this, I'll never forget."

"Hopefully we won't forget the moves either. I was thinking, if we want to show off our skills at the dance tomorrow night, we might need to practice one more time. Are you free in the afternoon?"

I reached for my planner on the mantel. I was learning—finally—to check my calendar before I made commitments. And it was a good thing that I did.

"Oh, I can't," I told Alex. "I'm stuck doing setup for the dance. I missed the committee meeting the other day, so it's Willa's form of punishment," I explained. "But it's actually going to be fun, because all the girls are going to come and help out."

"Ah, girl time, I get it," Alex said, looking disappointed. "They say you're not supposed to get jealous of your girlfriend's girlfriend time—"

"You," I said, putting my arms around him in the doorway, "have absolutely no reason to be jealous of my girlfriends. Practically all we do these days is gush about our boys. As soon as you show up at the dance," I promised, "I'll be all yours."

"I'm going to hold you to that," he said. We

kissed good night and I watched Alex walk down the steps.

It was only after I had shut the door that I realized I'd completely forgotten to give Alex his Valentine's Day present!

Chapter 22

DO A LITTLE DANCE, SHED A LITTLE TEAR, STORM OUT TONIGHT

Luckily, I'd get the chance to give Alex his gift less than twenty-four hours later. I couldn't wait to see the look on his face when he opened it. By Friday afternoon, the little wrapped box was tucked in my oversize Chanel trunk—the only thing I owned big enough to cart around the *five* formal dresses I'd scored from Jade Moodswing.

When I'd texted the girls last night to meet me at the Rainbow Room to set up two hours before the dance—and to agree to let me dress them—not one of them had put up a fight. I felt reassured by their complete fashion trust. Hopefully it meant that they were feeling equally as confident about the dates I'd found for them.

To help us get in the setup mood, we'd blared cheesy romance songs—fighting over whether to listen to another Jake Riverdale song (Camille) or to

Donovan (Morgan)—and we ordered in sushi from Onigashima. Morgan and I hung all the black-and-white blown-up prints that our photography class had taken, while Amory and Harper blew up balloons. Everything looked so picture-perfect, I was almost glad Willa had threatened to smear my reputation if I didn't show up to handle the grunt work. Popping the final spicy tuna roll in my mouth and surveying our finished product, I realized that the grunt work had actually been really fun.

"Okay, Flan," Camille said, straightening a matted print of the Hudson River Park that Morgan had taken. "That's the last of the romantic photo decorations. Now can we *please* see our Jade Moodswing dresses?"

"*Please*," all the other girls echoed.

They started oohing and ahhing before I'd even unlocked the trunk. And when I pulled out the first dress—a deep sapphire floor-length gown, all four of them started screaming.

"I was thinking this one for Harper," I said, holding up the dress against her skin. "To accentuate her dramatic clavicles."

"Perfect," Morgan agreed. "She is so the muse of Trevor's dreams."

For Morgan, I pulled out a puffy, tea-length gown in a pretty shade of rose quartz. "Jade called this one the New Love dress," I said. I'd picked it for Morgan, my ex-bitter friend who'd spent all week forwarding me cute texts from Bennett. It was strange, because I'd never really seen that side of him, but I quickly shrugged that off, just happy that Morgan had found someone to get excited about.

As for Camille, all day she'd been a little blasé about her date with Saxton, but once I pulled out the dramatically sleek, backless emerald silk dress, there was no denying the excitement on her face.

"Okay, this just made everything worthwhile!" she said, hugging me, then rushing to slip into the dress.

Finally, for Amory, I doled out an amber-colored gown with a keyhole neckline. "Sheesh," she said, fanning herself when she saw it. "Is it hot in here, or is it my dress?"

Good—that was the reaction I'd been going for. Of all my girls, Amory was the only one I was slightly worried about. She'd totally dismissed the idea of any of Feb's Aussie model friends, claiming Phil to be her one and only valentine. I hadn't been able to bring myself to confess everything to her, so my new plan was to quit stressing, keep my distance from Phil, and find Amory a dress that Phil wouldn't be able to take his eyes off of. At least the dress part of the plan was taken care of. . . .

"That's it," I said happily. "Is everyone satisfied with her couture?"

"*Absolument*!" Camille said, crossing her legs à la Jade Moodswing. "But why are you holding out on us? We need to see your gown *immédiatement*."

When at last I slipped into the brilliant opal ball gown, all my friends stopped fastening their own dresses to applaud. I loved that it fit me so well that I didn't even need a zipper.

"It's perfect," Harper said. "Alex is totally going to flip."

"That's the idea," I said, glancing down at my watch. "Speaking of which—he should be here any minute. In fact, all of our dates should. I'm going to go downstairs and wait for mine."

I tucked Alex's gift under my arm and took the looong elevator ride back down to earth. I couldn't wait to see him.

But apparently I was going to have to.

Ten minutes passed and he still wasn't there. Just before seven, several limos full of my formally clad classmates started showing up—including Sally, formerly known as Simone, formerly known as SBB. She was flying solo—I guess JR would have blown her cover—but she still arrived in the car with Willa and Kennedy.

As I tried not to fume, we exchanged icy stares as she passed. The vibe between us was as frigid as the weather, and neither one of us wanted to make the first thaw-out gesture.

Twenty minutes passed.

Standing alone on the curb in the freezing wind, I greeted Trevor and Saxton and even said a quick downward-gazing hello to Phil, who seemed to be avoiding my eyes too.

Still no Alex. Where was he? I'd left my phone in my bag, but it was all the way upstairs, and I didn't want to cross paths with him in the elevator if he showed up in the meantime.

I felt a familiar hand on my arm. *Finally*.

"There you are," I said, turning around.

Whoops—it wasn't Alex. It was Bennett.

I couldn't help it—my heart picked up. What was wrong with me?

"I was wondering," he said awkwardly. Uh-oh, was he going to ask me something about . . . us? Gulp.

"Have you seen Morgan?" he finally stammered.

"Oh," I said. "Sure, she's upstairs, I think—"

"Great, I'll go find her."

Just then a giant gust of wind knocked loose one of the primary bobby pins in my updo, and my formerly intricate braided bun came cascading down my shoulders. I was still holding Alex's present and didn't want to lose it in this wind, but I also didn't want to lose that bobby pin!

"Bennett," I called to him. "Can you help me? Just grab that bobby pin before it blows away?"

Bennett reached toward me as another gust of wind blew my hair all into my lip gloss. I hated that.

"Oh no," I said, trying to spit it out. "Help!"

"I'm trying," he said, brushing my hair out of my eyes. When he finally got it under control, I had spit all over him and he was holding my hair up in a mass above my head with both his hands. Our eyes met and we both started laughing.

An angry throat-clearing noise from behind us broke our moment.

Whoops. It was Morgan, and her face looked about as flushed as her gown.

"So it's true," she said. "I just overheard Sally talking about how the two of you used to date! Now I come downstairs to *this* scene? Nice matchmaking, Flan."

"Morgan, wait—" Bennett called, running after her.

It was then that I spotted Alex, who had picked the most inopportune instant of all instants to show up.

"Wow," he said, shaking his head. "I feel like such an idiot. Last night you were telling me how I shouldn't be jealous of the time you spent with your girlfriends. You didn't mention that I needed to watch out for your ex-boyfriends." He turned back to his town car and opened the door.

"Alex—it's not what you think!" I called, but he was already inside the car.

"I don't really feel like dancing anymore," he said, rolling up the window and driving away.

I was devastated. I looked down at the present I'd been holding out to give him—the very box that had caused this whole mix-up with Bennett and this stupid windstorm in the first place.

I couldn't believe that in thirty seconds, so much had fallen apart. I could either chase Alex's car down the street in my heels (not likely), or I could race upstairs to get my phone to call him—while simultaneously convincing Morgan that what she'd seen just now was *so* not what it had seemed.

After what felt like a year, I finally made it to the top floor and stepped back into the Rainbow Room. I couldn't even appreciate how elegant the place looked or how many of my fellow classmates were totally kicking it on the dance floor. I grabbed my bag from where I'd left it behind the bar and headed toward the ladies' bathroom. If I knew Morgan, she'd be there.

When I swung open the door, Morgan *was* there

(like I expected) crying (also like I expected) but she was flanked (*unexpectedly*) by Amory and Harper, who looked really pissed off.

Geez, the rumor mill must have been working faster than the elevator.

"Morgan—you have to believe me, nothing is going on with me and Bennett. It's so obvious that he's crazy about you."

"And it's so obvious that it drives *you* crazy. If you were over him, you would have told me that you guys had a history."

I looked to Amory for backup. She was always the voice of reason when my other friends got overdramatic. But she had daggers in her eyes for me as well.

"Don't look at me," she said. "You made such a big deal about picking the perfect dates for us all. If mine was so perfect, why did he ditch me for *your* friend Sally?"

"What?" I asked, my head spinning with the latest development.

"Trevor's been all over Sally too," Harper huffed. "It's hard for us to see how you didn't have a hand in all of this."

"You guys aren't being fair," I pleaded. "Where's Camille?"

"She bailed," Harper said. "She thinks Saxton is

totally boring and superficial. Is that the kind of guy you think is deserving of your friend?"

Looking at the three of them splayed out on the bathroom floor, part of me wanted to grovel at their feet, make up for this whole mess, and get their advice on how to dig myself out of trouble with Alex. The other part of me was furious.

"You've got to be kidding me," I said. "I have spent every waking minute of the last two weeks trying to make *you* guys happy—so we could all have a fun time tonight. I went through multiple Rolodexes for you guys. I hauled a giant trunk of couture across town so *you* could look fabulous tonight. I've been wearing myself to the bone for you all and this is how you repay me?"

The girls looked at one other and started to stand up and gather their things. "Don't bother storming out on my account," I said, ready to make an exit myself. "I'll save you the trouble."

Chapter 23

WHAT'S A PITY PARTY WITHOUT PIZZA?

After a long, sleepless night, I lay in bed early Saturday morning, listening to the rain. I was feeling really low. I knew it couldn't have all been a bad dream, because I'd been tossing and turning all night. And when the doorbell rang this time, I was pretty sure it wasn't a flower delivery from Alex again.

After a few more insistent rings of the bell, I grudgingly climbed out of bed and headed down the stairs.

"Whoever this is had better have a really good excuse," I muttered under my breath.

"Hey kiddo," a familiar voice said when I opened the door. It was Patch, looking almost as sleep-deprived and tousled as me. "Sorry to wake you—I forgot my keys."

Before I could formulate a coherent sentence, I had burst into tears and flung myself into his arms.

“My life is over,” I wailed. “All my friends and my boyfriend hate me.”

“Oh boy,” Patch said. “Sounds like we need air hockey and a large pizza from John’s.”

“Patch, it’s seven-thirty in the morning,” I said.

“Never too early for a pity party,” he said, grabbing my coat from the closet and helping me into it. “A pajama pity party is even better,” he said, taking in my attire as he sent a quick text.

I couldn’t believe I was going out like this, but at this point, it wasn’t like I had anything to lose. I followed my big brother across town to Ace Bar, his longtime favorite hangout in the East Village. The place was dingy and empty, and they didn’t care if you had a pizza delivered while you played. And if you were Patch Flood, they didn’t care if you texted two hours after they’d closed and said you were dropping by. Patch ordered a large pepper-and-mushroom pie and gave me a wad of singles to get quarters from the machine.

By the time we’d finished two games of air hockey (Patch and I were one and one), I’d spilled the whole story of the dance disaster. He hadn’t said much yet, but he was being a really good listener. We paused in quiet contemplation and dug into the giant floppy slices. It was sort of amazing that pizza could still work its wonders so early in the morning.

"So how do I get my friends back? And what do I do about Alex? And BTW, how am I related to someone who eats the crusts first?" I said, handing Patch my crust so I could move on to another cheesy slice.

"The chick-fight thing isn't exactly my turf, little sis. Don't girls usually just make up with retail therapy?" He polished off the slice and slipped another couple of quarters into the pinball machine. "As for the romance trouble, I probably shouldn't be giving out advice there, either."

"Oh no," I said, feeling stunned. "You and Agnes broke up?"

"She didn't like that I needed a little bit of space every now and then. I guess I didn't do a good enough job convincing her that just because sometimes I had to eat and sleep and have conversations with other people, that didn't mean I wasn't crazy about her." He looked out the dirty window. "Does that sound crazy?"

I couldn't believe my big brother was asking me for relationship advice. Patch looked more pensive than I'd ever seen him. Part of me wanted to be compassionate, but another part of me just had to take advantage of his mood and score on him to win the game. This was definitely a morning of firsts for us.

"One thing is clear," I said, after Patch had recovered from his loss. "Both of us are going to have to do some serious groveling if we want to get them back."

"Doesn't quite seem like a Flood thing to do, does it?" Patch said, slurping up the last of his Coke.

"Maybe not, but we're bingeing on pizza and bad arcade games before nine a.m.," I said. "We're pretty pathetic without them."

"Speak for yourself," Patch teased. "This is totally normal behavior for me."

"You know what?" I said.

"I think we should get out of here and start the long groveling process," Patch finished for me.

I nodded.

"This might be the first time we've agreed on something." I laughed.

"Good luck," Patch said, messing up my hair again.

"You too. Keep me posted," I said.

I was eager to get to work fixing things with Alex. But first I was going to have to put on something other than these pajamas.

Back on the street, Patch gave me a fist bump before I hailed a cab back toward our house and he turned south toward Agnes's.

"Don't forget that Floods always get what they want," he called, zigzagging through traffic.

Fingers crossed that his brotherly advice was right.

When I got to my stoop, I spotted SBB sitting at the top of my steps. I had to do a double take before I realized that the girl sitting before me wasn't Sally, and it wasn't Simone. It was just my SBB.

She held up a doggie bag from EJ's, our favorite spot for brunch.

"Truce?" she asked.

I sighed. I was too tired to argue, too tired to explain that I'd already eaten, too tired to do anything but nod.

"Can we crawl into bed?" I asked.

"I thought you'd never ask," SBB said, racing me up the stairs.

Once we were tucked under the covers and tucking into our omelets, SBB looked at me with a devilish grin.

"What happened to you last night?" she asked. "You managed to miss all the drama."

I just about choked on a sautéed mushroom.

"Are you kidding? I thought I *was* the drama last night. What could I possibly have missed?"

"Oh, only that Willa's secret boyfriend secretly fell

for Willa's little protégé—that would be me—I mean, past-tense me. He basically accosted me in the coatroom. And when Willa came in to get her phone, she saw everything and *flipped.* Over a high school boy—can you imagine? No offense. Anyway, after that, Willa tried to engage me in a catfight, and it amounted to her yanking off my wig and exposing me in front of the whole class."

My head was spinning with all the details of her story. At least it sounded like my drama would *not* be the gossip everyone was talking about back at school.

Now I was just trying to figure out in what order all of these things had happened. If SBB had been unveiled early enough in the night—then maybe that would explain why Harper and Amory's dates had both been all over her.

"After that, it was only a matter of time before the paparazzi showed up. I ducked out before I could do any further damage," SBB said, wrapping up her story. She sighed. "So thus endeth my career as a high school student. But oh my God, what a thrill. Even though it ended sort of dramatically, overall it was such a good experience to add to the old repertoire. Have I mentioned that I love high school drama?"

"I'm glad *you* like it," I sighed. "My own drama was

a whole lot less fun last night. In fact, I'm pretty sure you're the only person in the whole school who's still speaking to me."

"And I don't even go to your school anymore," she chimed in.

"Yes, thank you for pointing that out," I said, offering Noodles the rest of my omelet. Either I was still full from the pizza, or I'd lost my appetite along with all my friends. "I'm just upset that my friends think I went behind their backs. They actually blamed me for their dates falling all over you. Like I can control what they do once they're at the dance."

"Whoops," SBB said. "Sorry about that. I was only trying to show them how we danced on the set of *Oh My Chocolate Pie* so they could try it out on their own dates. Sigh. I guess high school drama isn't all fun and games. Are you mad at me for drawing too much attention?"

"Of course not," I said. "You didn't do anything wrong. My Thoney friends said they trusted me, but it's plain to see now that they never did."

SBB got a funny look on her face and was quiet for a moment.

"Hello?" I waved in front of her face. "Anyone in there?"

"Oh," she said, sounding distracted, "I'm sure it'll

just work itself out. You guys can just all go shopping and make up over retail therapy."

What? Now she was sounding like Patch. That advice was so unrealistic—and unhelpful. Was she turning back into Sally again or something?

"Well, I should probably get going," SBB said, quickly packing up the brunch plates and grabbing her bag. "Now that I'm not in high school anymore, I have time to catch up on the rest of my life. Have a great day, Flan! Let's do lunch soon."

She disappeared more quickly than she could change costumes and before I knew it, I was back in my room alone.

I hated to break it to SBB but she was definitely going to have to work on that empathy thing some more. But before I could harp on how even more alone I felt after her visit, I finally fell into a fitful sleep.

Chapter 24

THE MATCHMAKER GROVELS

By Sunday afternoon, I knew I needed to pull myself together. I'd have to face my friends at school the next morning, and SBB/Simon/Sally wouldn't even be there for me to fall back on for moral support. Since I knew I'd feel much better equipped to make up with my girlfriends if I could get over the sinking feeling in my stomach related to the recent loss of my boyfriend, I decided to swallow my pride and try calling Alex—for the sixth time.

After the dance on Friday night, I'd texted him a few times but still hadn't heard back. I wasn't sure how many more apologetic voice mails I could leave, but I tried to remember what Patch had said. *Floods always get what they want.*

Okay, I told myself in the mirror, *I'm going to give it one more try.*

WILL YOU JUST GIVE ME A CHANCE TO EXPLAIN? I texted.

This time, the reply was instantaneous.

STEP OUTSIDE AND GIVE IT YOUR BEST SHOT.

What? After the hell of the last few days, this seemed too good to be true. Still, when I went out to the hallway and looked out at the street, the Prince's town car was stalled outside of my house.

I rushed downstairs.

"What are you doing here?" I asked, unable to decide whether my heart was racing because I was nervous or excited.

"*Not* giving you a chance to explain," he said.

"But—"

"Why waste time?" he shrugged. "I've already forgiven you. I think I might have overreacted on Friday night. What do you say we forget about it and go grab some hot dogs?"

"Umm, I say—" *Thank god!* "I say, let me just grab one more thing before we go."

I didn't know where the afternoon would take us, but I did know that I wasn't going to miss another opportunity to give Alex his gift. I grabbed my bag and slipped the little box inside.

"You might want to bring your heavy scarf," Alex said, pointing at the sky. "It feels like snow outside."

When the town car dropped us off at the world's best hot dog stand, I could tell Alex was right. There was that electricity in the air that usually meant a rare Manhattan snowfall. I gripped his hand with excitement. It felt so good to have him back—almost too good to be true.

"I know it's freezing," he said, rubbing my hands as we waited for our two hot dogs with extra relish. "Should we get these to go and eat them in the car?"

I shook my head. "We can't go inside now. There's nothing better than being in Central Park to catch the first few flakes of snow."

Alex gave me that you're-kinda-insane-but-I-like-it smile and we grabbed a seat on the bench to dig into our hot dogs. It was pretty amazing how much better food tasted now that the giant lump in my throat had dissolved and I could actually swallow it.

"So can I ask what made you forgive me?" I said. "I was sort of looking forward to this whole groveling act I'd worked up."

"You should file that act away in case you need it next time," he said, then nudged me. "I'm kidding." Alex looked down at his shoes and started swinging his feet. "Well, partially it was that I kept replaying that scene with you and that guy Bennett in my mind. I knew something about it wasn't right, but I couldn't put my finger on what it was. Then, last night, I was playing pool with Phil and Saxton, and Phil sort of came clean about the note he sent to you last week."

Oh, crap.

"I was pissed at first," Alex continued. "But when Phil told me how you reacted, how it was never even a question in your mind, I knew that my instinct about Friday night was right. I had to come make it up to you."

I breathed an enormous sigh of relief. "Well, you just about covered all of my groveling points anyway." I laughed.

"I'm sorry, Flan," he said, leaning in to give me a kiss.

"I'm sorry too," I said.

At that very moment, the first snow began to fall.

"Wow, it's like this is out of a movie," I said.

Alex held up a finger. "Just wait—" he said.

"Don't tell me," I guessed. "There's more?"

This time, I was ready to insist on being the one to top the perfect moment with my belated Valentine's gift.

But once again, before I could take it out of my bag, Alex was standing up and holding his hands out to me. "I need to whisk you away to a secret destination and I need you to not ask any questions."

"But what—"

"Uh-uh." He shook his finger at me. "That sounds suspiciously like a question." He held open the door to the town car. "Hop in."

"More ice cream?" I guessed.

"No questions," he said, shaking his head.

The car started rolling east, and as I looked excitedly out the window for clues about our destination, Alex thwarted me again by pulling out a blindfold.

He shrugged. "How can it be a secret destination if you know where we're going?"

I considered protesting, but I could tell from the look on his face that he was enjoying this whole game, and the truth was, I was kind of into the mystique of it too. I leaned my head forward and accepted my blindfolded fate.

When the car finally came to a stop, Alex hopped out and took my hand so I could stumble out too. Even blindfolded, I could tell that we were on the water, because the wind was really biting into our faces. I could also tell that we weren't alone—there was a buzz in the air that wasn't just the snow's electricity.

"When am I allowed to ask questions?" I said to Alex.

"Patience," Alex said, reaching around the back of my head to untie the blindfold. "Not yet, not yet."

Standing in front of me on a dock facing the East River were Camille, Morgan, Harper, Amory, and SBB dressed as herself.

Before I could ask questions, a small fleet of helicopters swooped down to land next to us on the dock. Their propellers were loud, but my friends were louder, and they all held out their hands and yelled, "SURPRISE!"

Chapter 25

CONSIDER THIS YOUR LOVEFEST

"Okay," Alex said. "Now you can ask questions."

I was perched in the cramped backseat of a helicopter, flying over the East River next to SBB, Camille, and Alex. From the devilish look of excitement on SBB's face, I had a guess that we were headed toward her palace. But for the life of me, I couldn't figure out why—or how all of my friends had agreed to come after the debacle on Friday night.

"Will someone just start from the beginning?" I said.

"Well, remember how I said I was playing pool with the guys—" Alex started to explain, but was quickly interrupted.

"Morgan and I were midfume at H&H the next morning and—" Camille said at the same time.

"Excuse me." SBB's loud stage chirp silenced the other two. "As the mastermind behind this operation,

I believe I've earned the right to speak first and freely. Agreed?"

The rest of the helicopter's occupants giggled and nodded.

"So . . ." SBB turned to me. "Remember my awkward shuffle out of your house yesterday?"

"I don't think I could forget it." I nodded. "That was definitely some Oscar-worthy awkwardness."

"I know," she sighed. "It was weird, and I'm sorry for that, but when I get an idea as good as this one, I need to act on it without hesitation. You know that. Carpe diem!" She straightened her sequined headband and took a deep breath. "I bailed on you yesterday because I realized that I could fix *everything*!"

She looked at Camille. "What you girls didn't know was that I'd promised to help Flan keep everyone's date's eyes on the right girl on Friday. But after what happened with Willa, and then my unmasking—er, unwigging, which really hurt by the way. *Never* glue on a wig. Anyway, things got a little out of control—"

"You're a movie star, guys have no choice but to fall all over you, say no more," Camille finished. "I'm just baffled that I didn't pick up on your true identity earlier." She shook her head. "Either I've been *way* self-involved this week—or you, my dear, are an excellent actress."

"Thank you," SBB said seriously. She turned back to me. "Anyway, I dropped the ball at the V-Day ball, I know, so when I heard the whole rundown from you the next morning, I knew I had to let your friends know that your intentions were always good."

"So she hijacked us yesterday and took us to Fig & Olive to explain," Camille filled in.

SBB shrugged. "I just told them over pink peppercorn soup how hard you'd been working to find everyone's perfect match. And that you were putting in all that effort while simultaneously trying not to blow my cover—no small feat. *And* you did it even after my short-lived foray to the axis of evil—whoops!" she rambled on. "Obviously, after it was all out in the open, everyone instantly forgave you."

"You went to my favorite restaurant without me?" I asked, thinking about how I loved to sit at the antipasto bar at the sleek Meatpacking restaurant. It was weird to imagine SBB and my Thoney friends making dinner plans sort of behind my back. "How did that play out? What did the other girls say?"

"It helped," Camille continued, "that Bennett called Morgan twenty times to grovel and reassure her that he only had eyes for her."

Hearing Camille say that, I thought I might have had a different reaction. But all I felt was relief. Finally, things were as they should be—and now I could just put all that weirdness with Bennett behind me.

When Alex put his hand on my knee, I knew he was the one I really wanted.

He leaned in and said, "While we're on the subject of groveling, you should probably also know that I convinced a very pathetically depressed friend of mine to go grovel in front of Camille," Alex said.

"Huh? Do you mean Saxton?" I asked, not so sure whether Camille would really be into that.

"Actually . . ." Alex looked at Camille and winked. "I mean Xander."

Camille turned beet red and started fiddling nervously with her hair.

"You and Xander got back together??" I squealed, looking at my friend, who was suddenly all nods and shyness.

That the best news I'd heard all day.

"So everything came together," SBB said, clapping her hands. "Just exactly as I planned. I'm in high school for what, a week? And I've already perfected the social graces."

We all laughed, and as the helicopter started to descend, I turned to SBB.

"I'm still a little jealous that you guys went to Fig & Olive without me," I said. "But I guess I'm glad it resulted in this. Wait," I said, finally taking in the fact that we were landing on SBB's rooftop pad outside her palace in Long Island City. "What exactly *is* this?"

"Duh," SBB said as we touched down. "Don't you know about the only family tradition I have with Gloria?" she asked.

I shook my head.

"After every major blowout fight, we make up and have a lovefest," SBB said, as if it were common knowledge. "Remember our brawl after she got the same tattoo as me—and then my subsequent Sweet Fifteen birthday party in Cairo?" She shrugged. "Make-up lovefest."

Camille put her arm around my shoulder. "Consider this your we're-sorry-Flan lovefest," she explained. "SBB suggested we throw a party at her palace, and we all jumped to start planning."

"And don't worry," said Alex, who'd been awfully quiet. He gestured at my jeans and black turtleneck sweater. "We thought ahead. The Jade Moodswing dresses are waiting for you inside."

"Love that your boyfriend was the one to come up with that idea." Camille laughed.

"Me too!" I said, thinking about how important it was to have a good time in my opal dress so I wouldn't forever associate it with Friday night's drama.

Alex hopped out of the helicopter and helped each of us down to the windy patch of concrete. My hair was blowing all over the place, and I was still a bit overwhelmed by the forgiveness backstory I'd just been fed, but it didn't stop me from feeling like Cinderella being helped out of her carriage by the prince. It was definitely a moment deserving of a kiss.

"Someone pinch me," I said to Alex. "I'm worried that this is all a dream—or that the helicopter is going to turn into a pumpkin any minute or—"

"I'll give you a reality check." SBB gestured behind her. "Since you last visited the palace, I had a whole row of landing pads installed. Now up to ten helicopters full of revelers can land at a time. And Cinderella won't have to take the subway home—you can just stay a princess for good!"

Chapter 26

SNOWED OUT

Harper, Morgan, and Amory arrived on our heels in a second helicopter and twenty minutes later, my friends and I emerged from the ladies' lounge. We were reoutfitted in our Jade Moodswing jewel-tone dresses and ready to party. SBB had brought over her team of stylists to get us glammed up in a jiffy, and we were all sporting her newest fragrance, Starlet.

The palace looked amazing, with white leather couches and deep purple and gold lighting. JR's latest CD was blasting, and there were candles shaped like skyscrapers dotting the banquet tables and lining the catwalk.

Wow, I'd thought the Rainbow Room looked pretty swanky on Friday night, but this put our crepe paper, balloons, and matted photos to shame. The palace walls were even sporting some particularly notable décor from the Valentine's Dance: five of the NYC prints I was most proud of from my photography class.

Camille put her arm through mine. "We all put so much work into making the dance decorations really amazing. It seemed like a waste to abandon them even after most of us abandoned the dance." She shrugged. "So we asked SBB if we could use them here. It just seemed like the perfect match!" We stepped back to admire the black-and-white cityscapes hanging from the wall next to the real cityscape visible through the floor-to-ceiling windows.

"Okay you two," SBB said, grabbing our elbows and leading us over to the bar where Harper, Amory, and Morgan were waiting with flutes of champagne. "You can admire your own photographs later, Flan—"

"Hey!" I said.

"I'm kidding," SBB said, hands on her hips all mock indignant. "I've been admiring them all day! But right now, it's time for a toast."

I looked around for Alex. Where was he?

Reading my mind, Camille said, "Don't worry, he didn't go far. The rest of the party's about to arrive. Alex just went upstairs to let everyone in."

"And before all the boys show up, I want to propose a toast," SBB sang out.

We raised our glasses.

"To Flan," she said, "whose intentions are always good, even when her matchmaking choices are spotty."

There was a time when I would have taken this remark too seriously, but tonight, looking at all of my grinning, glamorous friends, I realized that I wasn't the only one who'd been through a lot this week. Even after all the drama, we'd come out smiling and with more than a few funny stories to tell.

"And to you guys," I said holding my glass out to clink. "For putting up with my obsessive matchmaking."

"You know what they say," Amory said. "Practice makes perfect. Even though Phil turned out to be a total frog, I can't say I minded kissing him to find that out."

Modest little Harper's jaw dropped, and Camille slugged her playfully on the shoulder.

"Don't act all prude, Miss Blueblood. You were totally pimping out your clavicles to Trevor just because he claimed to be an *artiste*!"

I busted out laughing and said, "Okay, okay, so Trevor and Phil and Saxton were lame. But look at Morgan and Bennett. My track record's not *all* bad. In fact, if anyone wants to go out with a really cute Australian guy, I could set it up—"

"NO!" All my friends cried at once, but all of us were laughing.

"Point taken." I shrugged. "Cheers."

"I çan see we're right on time," Alex's voice called from the doorway. Bennett and Xander and JR were all next to him, along with a few guys I sort of recognized as Daltonites but didn't really know.

"Is there enough champagne to go around?" Xander asked.

"At our palace," SBB said proudly, snuggling up to JR, "there is always enough champagne."

The guys filed in and everyone took a glass. The room was heating up with chatter and expensive formal wear.

"Omigod," Amory whispered. "That's Jason James. He's JR's costar from *Demolition Dudes*. Huge obsession. How's my hair?"

"Flawless," Harper assured her. "And isn't that Rick Fare, the tennis player? I think he goes to my country club."

Camille looked at me. "Our friends might not need your matchmaking anymore, but I must admit, the whole experience worked wonders to lift the boy boycott."

Xander was at her elbow. "I nabbed you a lamb chop lollipop," he said, looking proud of himself. "There were only a few left on the tray, and I know they're your favorite."

Camille grinned and snapped up the hors d'oeuvre. "Actually, there is something I like even more than lamb chops," she said flirtily. "Wanna dance?"

Speaking of dancing . . . I spotted Alex sitting at a booth next to SBB and JR and sank down next to them.

"There you are." He put his arm around me.

"You guys," I said, "this party is amazing. And this place looks incredible. SBB, how did you do it so quickly?"

SBB shrugged. "Jade Moodswing's personal assistants were desperate for work after she went back to Paris. I just made a call. She definitely trained them well: at the first mention of the party being in your honor, they got down to work like busy little worker bees. I'll have to send Jade a thank-you gift," she said, pulling out her BlackBerry to make a note.

Speaking of gifts, I was not going to wait any longer to give Alex his!

But just then, a waiter approached, bearing a giant red box tied with a white bow. "For Miss Flood," he said. "Special delivery."

I looked at Alex, but he just shrugged. In fact, he looked a little uncomfortable. Oh no, I *really* hoped this wasn't another valentine from an unwanted admirer. But everyone's eyes were on me—I had to open it.

Nervously, I broke the seal on the envelope, but

when I opened the card and saw the familiar handwriting, I breathed a giant sigh of relief.

I hate to miss a Valentine's Day with my favorite youngest daughter. Here's a token to help you capture it until I can get the full report!

Love,

Dad

Inside the box was the new Nikon camera I'd been admiring for months. It probably wouldn't have occurred to me that I needed a replacement for the battered old camera I'd been using, but now I was super psyched to trade up, thanks to Dad. And when I showed Alex the card, he looked even more relieved than I was.

"Well, I guess I can share you with your family," he joked. "Now, I hope you won't be too embarrassed, but I asked the DJ to play the salsa song we practiced to the other night. Do you still remember the moves?"

"You lead," I said. "I'll, uh, try to follow."

After JR's hip-hop song came to a smashing close, the familiar music came on and I could hear Paco's shouts in my head. My heart started racing. I really didn't want to be accused of having elephant feet again, especially not on an empty dance floor in front of all my friends!

But when Alex put his arm around my waist, all the moves came right back to me. Soon we were spinning around the parquet floor. I was grinning and a little dizzy, but then I reminded myself that Alex made me feel like that most of the time, even off the dance floor. Before I knew it, the music had ended and I looked around at all my applauding friends.

"Encore!" Camille shouted.

It was a little embarrassing, a lot exhausting, but mostly it was just a blast.

Alex and I slid into some open seats by the bar and ordered two large ice waters to catch our breaths.

"Breaking news," JR said, coming up behind us with SBB. "The weather just got too wild to fly anyone home. Looks like we're going to have to keep this party rocking till broad daylight."

I looked out the windows and couldn't believe my eyes. I'd been having so much fun I hadn't even realized how hard the snow was coming down. I also couldn't believe it was already midnight.

"Oh, these pilots *claim* they don't want to fly until it calms down for so-called safety reasons." SBB gestured over at her fleet of sexy dark-haired pilots. "Personally, I think they just don't want the party to end," she said. "You should see how much caviar they've eaten!"

"Either way," Alex said, leading me over to the windows to watch the snow, "I can't think of anyplace I'd rather wait out a storm."

Chapter 27

FLYING HIGH

It was a good thing that most of the partygoers agreed with Alex, because the snow didn't let up until almost sunrise.

We rocked the dance floor pretty hard until about three in the morning, but eventually exhaustion caught up with everyone. Well, almost everyone.

Bennett and Morgan were huddled near the bar, gazing into each other's eyes and having a heart-to-heart. But Camille and Xander had passed out on the lounge next to window, and Amory, Harper, and their newfound crushes looked like sardines, sleeping in a row on the catwalk. SBB and JR were wearing matching sleep masks and had changed into matching gray Ralph Lauren pajamas. Even I, who had a hard enough time sleeping in the world's most comfortable bed, found myself dozing on Alex's shoulder.

By five-thirty, he was shaking me awake.

The helicopter pilot was standing over us.

"The storm's letting up. You guys want to take the first flight back to the city? Best view in the world."

Alex and I looked at each other and shrugged. How could we argue with that?

I went over to the sleeping SBB and planted a kiss on her forehead. "Thank you for everything," I said. "Thank you for being SBB."

"It's Sally," she murmured in her sleep. She was going to have to break the habit soon enough.

I laughed and took Alex's hand as we walked out to the roof.

The city had never looked so beautiful. As the last few flakes fell around us, the gray glint of sky behind us started to glow a pinky yellow. Thick, powdery snow coated the treetops and cars below us. Even the East River looked shockingly pristine.

"It's so quiet," I whispered.

"It's so perfect," Alex said, taking my hand as we took off. "Look out there, near the Fifty-ninth Street tram. I think I see a raven's nest—that's a-mazing."

"Wait," I remembered. I was glad that I finally got to be the one to say, "There's more."

When I reached into my tote to reveal a gold-wrapped gift with a bow the size of the small box, Alex's eyes lit up.

"I didn't get to give this to you on Valentine's Day," I explained. "Or at the dance, or at the hot dog stand. I'm not going to let another minute go by."

"You didn't have to get me anything, Flan."

"Yeah, right!" I said. "You have no idea how much I stressed over what to get for you—or what I bought initially and had to return when I came to my senses." I shuddered, remembering the mocket, which seemed like years ago. "But when this idea came to me, I knew you were going to love it."

Slowly, Alex unwrapped the box. As soon as he pulled out the compact pair of binoculars I'd special ordered from GRDN, a hipster nature store in Park Slope, a huge grin spread across his face.

"Do you have any idea how long I've been wanting these?" he said, holding up the binoculars to his eyes.

"Only about as long as that red-tailed hawk's been in Manhattan," I guessed. "Look," I said, gesturing to the box. "There's even more!"

Alex pulled out the Audubon *Birds of America* guidebook I'd bought him to go with the binoculars.

"I hope you won't regret giving me this," he joked. "I'm going to be dragging you back to the park all the time to go bird-watching now."

"As long as there are hot dogs involved, I won't mind at all."

We were flying directly over the park then, and Alex held the binoculars to my eyes so I could look down. The view of the barely waking-up city was unbelievable—and the binoculars were pretty sweet too.

Soon the helicopter started dipping back down near the Hudson River piers. I couldn't believe our spectacular sunrise flight was coming to an end.

"Before we land, there's one more thing," Alex said, reaching under his feet. "I didn't get a chance to give you my gift yet either."

He pulled out a long, thin shiny silver-wrapped box, which I promptly tore into.

"Oh my gosh," I gasped, catching a glimpse of the corner. Even before I'd fully unwrapped it, I knew exactly what it was.

It was a framed print of the Spanish watercolor of the tidal wave that we'd been admiring at the Guggenheim last week. I'd always wanted to buy some of the artist's work to hang in my room. This was even more special because now I could think of Alex every time I looked at it.

"Do you know what I think?" I asked Alex.

"What?" he said, taking my hand.

"I think these gifts are the perfect match."

"Kind of like another duo I know," he said. My perfect match leaned in to give me the perfect kiss. The helicopter had just touched back down on solid ground, but I was pretty sure I was still flying.

DON'T MISS A MINUTE OF FLAN'S FABULOUS LIFE—

"I wish I'd known Flan Flood in high school—and not just because she has a hot older brother with hot older friends (although that totally helps). Don't let the name fool you—this is one girl you must get to know, now." —Lisi Harrison, author of the #1 *New York Times* bestselling series The Clique